# "Have I Proved Myself, Your Highness?"

Jaw as tight as the rest of him, Alex released her. "You are very bold, Sophia."

She nodded. "I'm going in now. You'll be all right out here by yourself?"

"I always have. I always will."

Alex saw her flinch slightly before saying, "Good night, then."

He watched her go, all the way up the sandy beach and into the house. His mind was blistered from their silly game of seduction. But it wasn't merely madness and unrequited pleasure that plagued him. Those two shackles he could deal with.

No, it was something far more dangerous.

For the first time in six years, he felt connected with life—open to lust, to need, to pain and to want.

And Sophia Dunhill was his keeper of the keys....

Dear Reader,

Welcome to another stellar month of stories from Silhouette Desire. We kick things off with our DYNASTIES: THE BARONES series as Kristi Gold brings us *Expecting the Sheikh's Baby* in which—yes, you guessed it!—a certain long-lost Barone cousin finds herself expecting a very special delivery.

Also this month: The fabulous Peggy Moreland launches a brand-new series with THE TANNERS OF TEXAS, about *Five Brothers and a Baby,* which will give you the giddy-up you've been craving. The wonderful Brenda Jackson is back with another story about her Westmoreland family. *A Little Dare* is full of many big surprises…including a wonderful secret-child story line. And *Sleeping with the Boss* by Maureen Child will have you on the edge of your seat—or boardroom table, whatever the case may be.

KING OF HEARTS, a new miniseries by Katherine Garbera, launches with *In Bed with Beauty*. The series focuses on an angel with some crooked wings who must do a lot of matchmaking in order to secure his entrance through the pearly gates. And Laura Wright is back with *Ruling Passions,* a very sensual royal-themed tale.

So, get ready for some scintillating storytelling as you settle in for six wonderful novels. And next month, watch for Diana Palmer's *Man in Control*.

More passion to you!

*Melissa Jeglinski*

Melissa Jeglinski
Senior Editor, Silhouette Desire

Please address questions and book requests to:
Silhouette Reader Service
U.S.: 3010 Walden Ave., P.O. Box 1325, Buffalo, NY 14269
Canadian: P.O. Box 609, Fort Erie, Ont. L2A 5X3

# Ruling Passions
## LAURA WRIGHT

Published by Silhouette Books
**America's Publisher of Contemporary Romance**

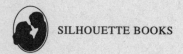 **SILHOUETTE BOOKS**

ISBN 0-373-76536-3

RULING PASSIONS

Copyright © 2003 by Laura Wright

This edition published by arrangement with Harlequin Books S.A.

® and TM are trademarks of Harlequin Books S.A., used under license. Trademarks indicated with ® are registered in the United States Patent and Trademark Office, the Canadian Trade Marks Office and in other countries.

Visit Silhouette at www.eHarlequin.com

**Printed in U.S.A.**

**Books by Laura Wright**

Silhouette Desire

*Cinderella & the Playboy* #1451
*Hearts Are Wild* #1469
*Baby & the Beast* #1482
*Charming the Prince* #1492
*Sleeping with Beauty* #1510
*Ruling Passions* #1536

# *LAURA WRIGHT*

has spent most of her life immersed in the world of acting, singing and competitive ballroom dancing. But when she started writing romance, she knew she'd found the true desire of her heart! Although born and raised in Minneapolis, Laura has also lived in New York City, Milwaukee and Columbus, Ohio. Currently, she is happy to have set down her bags and made Los Angeles her home. And a blissful home it is—one that she shares with her theatrical production manager husband, Daniel, and three spoiled dogs. During those few hours of downtime from her beloved writing, Laura enjoys going to art galleries and movies, cooking for her hubby, walking in the woods, lazing around lakes, puttering in the kitchen and frolicking with her animals. Laura would love to hear from you. You can write to her at P.O. Box 5811 Sherman Oaks, CA 91413 or e-mail her at laurawright@laurawright.com.

To my child, who grows inside of me
as I write this final Fiery Tale: Daddy and I love you.

# Prologue

The sea took the shape of a woman's hip as it climbed into a wave: curved and pink in the setting sun. But Crown Prince Alexander William Charles Octavos Thorne had no use for women anymore, real or imagined.

Lungs filled with salty air, he sagged against a jagged rock and watched the surf crash against the beach and crawl toward him.

He didn't run from its progress, didn't move. Not even when icy water stung his foot.

He understood the sea's endless need to consume, to take, to hurt. For five long years he'd felt the like— too many times to count. Then there was today...

Three hours ago he'd received word that his wife had left town, left him for another man. Like the cold, pinkish waves before him, relief rippled through his blood. Relief and anger—for a woman who'd hated him the minute they'd married, a woman who'd acted like a bloody iceberg no matter how hard he'd try to care for her, a woman who'd wanted no children, no warmth, no friendship.

Alex tore off his shirt, let the cool air rush over his chest.

He'd been a man of his word, married a woman he'd hardly known, remained loyal and honorable to her, kept silent when she'd told his father and the court that they were trying to conceive a child—even kept up the charade that they'd been living together for the past two years.

But today, on the day she'd run off with another man, loyalty, honor and care went to Llandaron only. Alex had his country to think of now, damage control to see to. If the world found out the truth of his situation, the heart of the Llandaron people could be destroyed forever.

Pretense was his only saving grace.

He would move slowly, tread easily. He would use whatever money and means was required to settle this matter, while keeping the truth hidden for as long as possible. Next week he left for his summit in Japan with the emperor. He would make his wife's excuses, take care of business, and while he was there, call in a favor from an old school chum he trusted, who just happened to be a divorce barrister in London. Then at some point, he'd return home to Llandaron and tell his family—tell his father that he'd failed.

At that offensive realization, Alex's jaw tightened to the point of pain. If there was anything he despised more than failure it was admitting it.

Echoing his mood, twilight seeped in around him and the sea turned choppy, each boundless curl morphing from pale pink to violent purple.

From this day forward, he vowed silently, no woman would rule him.

And from this day forward, the prospect that he would rule dimmed.

The lifelong assumption that he would govern his country might now have to be put aside in favor of his brother, Maxim. For a queen and an heir were vital to the Kingdom of Llandaron. And Maxim had both.

Pain snapped at Alex's heart. He opened his mouth and released five years of unlivable ache. The gut-wrenching cries to the sea echoed, ricocheting back into his ears, making him start, stop.

Suddenly his eyes widened, focused. All thought drifted down, sank into the wet sand under his feet as out in the distance, a sailboat lurched across the coarse sea.

For one brief moment, before the boat disappeared behind the towering cove walls, he saw a woman, perched on the bow of the craft like one of the jewel-tailed mermaids from his childhood dreams, all mind-blowing curves and brazen, red hair.

She was facing him, her long hair thrashing about her neck and chest like silken whips. She seemed to stare straight at him—a bizarre sensation, as her eyes were impossible to make out. Unlike the delectable combination of senses emanating from her: air, water and fire.

From gut to groin Alex went hard.

A massive wave crashed just inches from him, spitting saltwater into his face, his mouth and eyes. He scrubbed a hand over his face to clear the mist, then quickly glanced up.

Both boat and mermaid were gone.

Awareness, raw and demanding battled in his blood, but he shoved the feeling away. He'd felt need before, perhaps not this strong, but he'd fight it just the same. No woman would rule him.

Jaw set, Alex stripped bare and dove into the frigid water, determined to remind the lower half of him—just as he had his mind—who was master.

# One

---

*Llandaron*
*Four months later*

Fog surrounded the sloop like a perilous curtain, while the influx of seawater slithered into the hull in a snake-like stream.

As she stuffed wet couch cushions into the cavity, Sophia Dunhill cursed herself for forgetting to plot her estimated position.

How could she have been so stupid? So scattered?

Maybe because with her grandfather's beautiful homeland in her sights, all thoughts of navigation had simply drifted from her mind.

She'd been sitting on the deck with the late-afternoon sun warming her shoulders, staring out at the small island nation just off the coast of Cornwall. She'd felt mesmerized by Llandaron. Her mountains and her beautiful landscape of trees, purple heather and rocks itching with beach grass.

The weather had been absolutely perfect. Blue sky, calm seas. Then everything had changed. Out of nowhere thick fog had rolled in like a milky carpet so fast she'd barely had time to think. And in seconds the *Daydream* had collided with the rocky coastline.

How was it possible? A sailor for a good ten years and she hadn't seen this one coming.

Panic surged in her blood as she bolted up the companionway steps to the deck and straight into the thick fog. She couldn't lose this vessel to her own stupidity and a pile of rock. It was all she had left of her grandfather. The beautiful sloop was his legacy, his dream—and the one thing that only they'd shared. It had to remain afloat. After all, she still had one leg of this voyage, her grandfather's voyage, to complete. She had to dock the *Daydream* in the small fishing village of Baratin where her grandfather was born before she could return home to San Diego, to her empty apartment and to the writer's block that had plagued her since his death.

Baratin wasn't far, just on the other side of Llandaron, and come hell or rough water she would make it.

With steady hands she hauled a spare sail across the deck and draped it over the gaping hole. But the water was too powerful. The padding wasn't going to hold for long. Especially bumping against the rocks the way they were.

A fleeting thought born out of panic, shot into her mind and she quickly shoved it away.

Abandon ship.

But to a sailor, abandoning ship was akin to abandoning a child. It wasn't done.

At that moment seawater burst through a deck plank like a geyser. The boat shifted, groaned in pain.

Abandoning her child.

Sophia's heart squeezed. She had no choice.

Grabbing the chart and ditch bag she'd packed, Sophia eased her way to the bow of the boat. Was she a coward to take the easy road? she couldn't help but wonder. For a moment she was reminded of her parents' funeral, of the decision she'd made that day to defy their will and go and live with her grandfather instead of her stern aunt Helen. After years of living with two domineering spirits, Sophia had felt desperate for freedom. She'd gone on instinct, and finding her grandfather had been one of the best decisions of her life.

Instinct was all she had to cling to now, and it was screaming at her to jump.

Sophia gave one last glance at the chart to make sure she knew which way to swim. Then, with her eyes closed, her breath a little too tight in her lungs, she listened for the sound of the waves just as her grandfather had taught her.

And after snugging up the straps on her life jacket, she slipped into the water.

He'd hoped to keep the world out.

At least for a while.

From the deck of his beach house, Alex Thorne leaned back in his chair, took a pull on his beer and reveled in the shroud of fog that enveloped him. Granted the mystical fog only lasted one hour in Llandaron. But it was an hour of no questions, no answers and it was pure ecstasy.

After returning home from London five days ago, there had been nothing but questions and the demand for answers. As always he'd dealt with each as succinctly and as nonemotionally as possible. His family didn't need details of his failed marriage, just the facts: he was divorced and back home to resume his duties, face his people.

Given his brusque nature, Alex had thought the news would flow easily from his lips. But it hadn't. Deep in his gut, shame had paved the road.

His brother, Maxim, and sister, Catherine, had offered their support and their love, while his father had listened with a tight expression, giving off only sighs and an occasional nod.

Alex didn't scorn the man's pragmatic reaction. In

fact, he understood it. He, too, was worried about Llandaron and how its citizens would take the news of his failure when it was soberly announced at the annual Llandaron Picnic on Saturday. He couldn't forget how year after year his people waited patiently for news of a child. News that would never come.

Could his people forgive him this, too? Or would they ask him to step down in favor of Maxim?

Alex took another pull on his beer and stared out into the fog-shrouded sea he bowed to whenever he needed some semblance of comfort. There was no getting past the fact that he loved his people more than his own life. And he was ready to do as they wished. Whatever they wished—

Suddenly, Alex stopped short, all thoughts spent, and leaped to his feet. Brow furrowed, he cocked his head to the side and listened.

A sound. A cry—coming from the water, faint, but desperate—echoed over the beach. A sound that made his blood run cold.

Gut in his throat, Alex bolted off the deck, dropped down onto the cool sand and raced to the water's edge. The fog was thick as butter, but the visual impasse didn't make him cautious. He could have run that stretch of beach blindfolded, he'd combed it so many times.

There it was again. A woman's cry. Louder now.

Without pausing to think, Alex thrashed into the

surf, then dove beneath the waves. He swam like a demon toward a cry muffled by the swirl of the sea.

When he surfaced, he fought for his bearings. He looked right then left, then behind himself as his legs worked like twin engines in the water.

It took all of five seconds for him to locate the source of that cry. Red hair, wide eyes, pale complexion. A woman thrashing about in the water, the strings of her life vest caught on rock.

Her shouts for help grew hoarse, weak. She was obviously tiring. The erratic tumble of Alex's heartbeat thumped in his ears as he swam like a sea snake straight for her. Once he reached her side, he wasted no time with words. He ripped the vest from the rock, then eased his arm around her waist and scooped her up.

But in his haste for shore, his leg caught, gripped by a colony of seaweed. The slimy mess wrapped his ankle like a hungry Octopus, dragging him down, dragging him under.

Cursing, he lost hold on the girl, for a moment lost his breath as he struggled under the whirling sea. Panic knocked him senseless as his pulse raced wildly in his chest. Floating below the surface of the green sea, he saw fleeting images of death, his death.

Then suddenly he felt a rush of water loop his legs, saw the red-haired woman down by his ankle, cutting him away from the slimy green god.

Up he sailed, practically flew to the surface of the

water like a helium balloon to the blue sky. Air smashed into his lungs. Coughing and sputtering, he fought to stay above the lurching sea.

Then, just when he thought fatigue might claim him, an arm eased across his chest, hooked him like a sad fish and he felt himself move.

The waves rose and fell around him like the footfall of a giant as they inched toward shore. The woman took her time, swimming slowly, taking the waves with gentle insistence, allowing them both a chance to get their bearings.

Though Alex's lungs ached, his breathing soon regulated and his pulse eased toward normal as he floated on the surface of the water.

By the time his feet hit wet sand, he could walk. But he didn't stay upright for long. When he felt the comfort of dry sand, he dropped down and stretched out. He heard the woman ease down beside him.

"You better be all right, Lancelot," she said breathlessly.

It took Alex a good thirty seconds to respond to the thoroughly American quip. "Lancelot?"

"The knight? The one who rushed in to save the damsel in distress?"

"Right," he mumbled, rubbing a hand over his wet face. "The one who rushed in to save the damsel in distress, then got his foot caught in the seaweed."

"Seaweed, stirrups…same difference." The woman put a hand on his shoulder. "You're okay, right?"

"I'll live." Alex forced his heavy eyelids open. "So, if I'm Lancelot that must make you…"

The words died on his lips. Framed in a halo of milky-white fog, just inches from his face, was a woman of such heavenly beauty he nearly thought he'd succumbed to the pull of the ocean depths. Eyes the color of the sea—pale green with tinges of blue—and miles of red hair, wet and in gentle waves.

His body tightened. It *was* her. He felt it in his bones—that same need, that same connection. How was this possible? The mermaid from four months ago, here. Washed up on his stretch of beach.

"I think that makes me an idiot," she said with dry humor. "Actually I'd say we're both idiots."

"How do you figure?"

"Me getting caught on that rock." She dragged her tongue across her lower lip thoughtfully. "You getting caught in the weeds."

If he snaked a hand around the back of her neck, pulled her down to him, would she part her lips for him, kiss him the same hungry way he wanted so desperately to kiss her? "That doesn't sound like idiotic behavior to me."

"No? What does it sound like, then?"

"Divine intervention. Perhaps we're both looking to get caught."

The fog seemed to suffuse Alex all at once. He had

no idea what had made him say such an insane thing, but it was too late to retract the statement.

The woman stared intently at him, as though she could see right through his skin. "I'm not looking to get caught, I'm looking to find freedom."

"God knows why, but right now they seem to be one and the same." He said the words as much to himself as to her.

Confusion swept her face. "Yes, they do. Why is that?"

She didn't give him a chance to answer, though he really had none to offer. This mood, this moment, was unreal, surreal. She lowered herself on top of him. Her arms snaked around his neck, her needful gaze melted into his own and she kissed his mouth. Just once, one soft, small touch.

Alex cursed the delicious weight of her, the fullness of her breasts pressing against his chest, the pouty lips just inches from his own.

With the fog as her refuge, she was doing something terrible and highly erotic to him, something he'd never felt before—or wanted to feel. Her eyes, the way she looked at him…she had him bound, deep in a trance—a mysterious, sensuous trance. And he needed to get lost there.

Mouth to mouth, body to body, fog blanketing them from the world. Pure paradise.

The freedom to be caught.

His pulse slammed her rhythm in his blood. This

had to be a dream. Or maybe it was a nightmare, he reasoned as pure heat came over him, dark and unstoppable. A nightmare where all the control he prided himself on was lost. Where his mind went, his reason, too.

Animal instinct took him. He shifted, had her on her back in seconds. He watched as she smiled tentatively, then lifted her chin, parted her lips. Was he insane? he wondered as her eyes drugged him, drew him in. Did he care?

The surge of need that rippled through him was completely foreign. Or maybe it had just been tucked away, waiting…

A deep, aching groan erupted from his throat as he lowered his head, brushed his lips over hers, just to test, to tease. And as he'd hoped, prayed, she met him.

Hot mouth, sweet tongue. Her fingers fisted in his hair, pulling him closer.

Alex couldn't think—didn't want to think. He whispered against her mouth, "What are we doing?"

With an erotic nibble on his lower lip, she uttered, "I have no idea. But it feels so good."

"Too good."

His mind went blank once again as she kissed him, deeply, urging him to follow, to play, to plunder. Total madness took him, and his kiss turned ravenous. She angled her head over and over, her hips pressing up, up against the steel in his jeans.

A need for control rapped at his mind. He pulled

away, just an inch, his eyes burrowing into hers. Sea-green hunger stared up at him, willed him to close his eyes and take—only take. And when a bleating cry of distress escaped her throat, he silenced her in the only way he knew how.

Around them, the ocean pounded the shore.

Around them, the fog swirled.

With a wildness he was just beginning to understand, she pulled at his T-shirt, fumbled with the button on his jeans. Then before he could think, she rolled them both over until she was straddling his waist, fog lacing her face.

Pulse pounding, Alex eased down her bathing suit top, cupped her full breasts in his palms, rolled the swollen buds between his thumbs and forefingers. A hot gasp rushed out of her, and he felt her quiver over and over against his erection. He knew she was on the brink of release, totally free to take what she wanted.

He tugged at her nipples as she moved her hips against him in a rhythm as timeless as the ocean waves. Beneath them, sand flicked and flew. Alex moved with her, taking her to the edge as against his fingers, those rosy peaks turned crimson.

Suddenly she cried out, a deep aching sound from low in her throat.

Painfully hard, Alex rolled her on her back. He had her suit off, her thighs splayed before the next ocean wave crashed against the beach behind them. Breath heavy, eyes hungry, she wrapped her long, glorious legs around him, then slammed her hips upward.

Alex stared down at her. "Do you want this?"

"Yes," she whispered, panting.

Without another word, another thought, Alex rose up and plunged inside of her. He gasped as she stretched around him, wet and hot. "You feel like heaven."

A moan escaped and the words, "I'm no angel." She lifted and lowered her hips, moving him in and out of her body with wild, wicked strokes.

Complete madness took him. But he knew the madness couldn't last long, and that made him sick with anger. He wanted to be lost in this, in her, in this hallucination forever. But his body was weak from years of denial.

Sweat beaded on his brow as he drove into her, burrowing them both deeper into the sand.

She was so tight. So was he.

Her hands were everywhere at once; his back, his buttocks, gripping his shoulders. Until she stiffened, her legs releasing their hold on him and opening wide.

He could feel her climax coming, rumbling through her body like thunder, grasping him with her muscles. The feeling was so sweet he thought he'd lose his mind.

But instead he lost his control.

And as she convulsed around him, tightening, squeezing, Alex gave in, fell over the edge and exploded along with her.

As the heat of Sophia's body ebbed, so did the fog around them. For one full minute she silently prayed that it would take her with it, up into the sky where it was safe from reality and awkwardness. But as she'd learned early in life, the elements kept their own counsel.

The man beside her shifted, his hot skin grazing her own.

Unbidden, her body stirred in response. She stifled a groan. No, she was no angel. Burying her face in her lover's neck, she wondered how in the world had she allowed such a thing to happen. Granted, she wasn't someone who shied away from life—but making love to a total stranger was completely over the top.

And, yet, she wanted more.

More lying naked beside the most achingly handsome man she'd ever seen. More time where loneliness and uncertainty subsided and wonderfulness abounded.

More feeling like a woman, desired and consumed.

Reaching twenty-six years old with one pale love affair to her credit, she'd often fantasized about moments like this. She just never imagined one becoming reality. And now that it had, waking up wasn't as easy as opening her eyes to the morning sunshine and

safety of her nautical bedroom back home in San
Diego.

Sophia's thoughts faded as the man beside her disentangled himself from her grasp and sat up. His jaw
was as tight as a lobster trap, his heather-colored eyes
filled with dismay as he looked down at her. Her heart
lurched and fell, and she felt very naked. Despite his
gloriously handsome features, his expression was one
of consternation.

But for his own actions or for hers, she wasn't sure.

With her cheeks turning pinker by the second, she
snatched up her bathing suit and hurriedly slipped it
on as she tried for a casual tone. "I suppose you
won't believe me if I say that I've never done anything like this before?"

His eyes were blank now, no banter, no smile. "I
must apologize."

His husky brogue washed over her, heating her skin
once again under her wet suit. "There's no reason for
an apol—"

"Of course there is." He cursed, drove a hand
through his thick, black hair. "You were practically
drowning out there—"

"So were you."

"—and I—"

"And we," she corrected.

He paused for a moment, his gaze moving over her.
"Who are you?"

A fool? she felt an impulse to exclaim. A shameless

woman with absolutely no hindsight. A woman so desperate to live a little, she'd lost her mind...for a moment. "Maybe it's better that we don't know each other's names."

He released a haughty snort. "Impossible."

"Not really. Don't ask. Don't tell." Just give me five minutes to disappear, she thought dryly.

"I'm afraid that rule doesn't apply here."

"Why not?"

He stood up then, slipped on his jeans, all broad shoulders and lean muscle. Lord, the man could've been carved in bronze he was so well put together. Wavy black hair licked the back of his neck, razor-sharp features showed off his imperious nature to perfection, and then there were those amethyst eyes—needful, yet proud as a lion.

"Let's just say I'm old-fashioned," he said dryly.

"Well, I'm not," she countered. It was a lie, but emotional anxiety always brought out the worst in her. She wasn't about to spill her guts to this man. Not when he was making it crystal clear that their lovemaking was a huge mistake. She wasn't going to tell him her name, where she was from, that she was sailing the isles for her grandfather as she tried to come up with a decent idea for her next children's book.

No. She just wanted to run.

"I don't want to resort to commands," he began,

crossing his arms over his thickly muscled chest. "But I will."

Sophia's brows shot together; she wasn't sure she'd heard him correctly. "Excuse me?"

"I'm afraid I will have to command you to tell me who you are."

"Command me?"

"That's correct."

She grinned, let out a throaty laugh and shook her head, the tension inside her easing considerably. "That's very funny. You're funny. So that must make you what? The king of Llandaron or something?"

He shook his head brusquely. "Not yet."

Her stomach pinged with nerves, but she shoved the feeling away, forced out another easy laugh. "Well then, I suppose you can call me the queen of the sea."

"This isn't a time for humor, Miss…"

"I agree." She stood up, straightened her shoulders. This was getting ridiculous. They'd acted without thinking, made a horrible mistake. But it was over. She needed to get out of here. Now. Before this charade went any further. Before she made an even bigger fool out of herself. "Any more commands before I go find a boatworks, sire?"

His severe gaze fairly wilted her resolve. "Just one."

She swallowed, feeling the heat in her belly fire to

life—and hating herself for such a reaction. "Knock yourself out."

"I was careless. For that I apologize."

"Please, no more apolo—"

"You may be carrying my child, miss... The heir to the throne of Llandaron." He raised a fierce brow at her. "I'm afraid you'll have to remain with me, in my kingdom, until I know for certain."

# Two

Alex watched the blood drain from the woman's beautiful face like wet paint from a canvas, and felt as though he wanted to ram his fist through a wall. He was the cause of the unease and shock she was feeling. He'd been too quick, too apathetic, in his quest to bring reality to the situation.

As though in the path of a rolling ball of fire, the woman leaped, glanced over her shoulder, then returned her stormy green gaze to him. "Listen, whoever you are. This, whatever it is, has gotten way out of hand."

Alex was calm as he replied, "You don't believe me?"

She sniffed, looked him up and down. "No, of course I don't."

"There are many ways to prove my identity."

"I'm sure there are," she said, her tone thick with agitated sarcasm. "But I'm not really up for more games today."

"Neither am I."

"Good." Her gaze filled with strength as her long, fiery hair swirled around them. "My boat hit a rock and is flailing around out there. I need to have it towed in before—"

"There's no need to worry about your boat. I will have it brought in for you."

"That's not necessary."

"I think under the circumstances—"

"Thank you, but I can handle it. Now if you'll excuse me." And with that she turned to leave.

But her hasty departure was something Alex couldn't allow. This was far from over, far from resolved. He grabbed her hand.

When she whirled back to face him, her expression screamed antagonism. "You've got some nerve, buddy."

A grin tugged at Alex's mouth. No one had ever spoken to him with such ferocity. Granted, she didn't believe he was the crown prince of the country, but still her pluck intrigued him.

"What do you plan to do while you wait for the repairs on your boat?" he asked.

She tugged her hand from his. "I haven't made any immediate plans yet."

Alex looked out toward the ocean, saw the boat thrashing around and made a quick assessment. "With damage like that, repairs will take a few weeks at the very least."

"We'll see. I'm pretty good with boats, so maybe I'll lend a hand."

"I don't think Mr. Verrick will allow such a thing, but of course, there is no harm in trying."

"Thanks for the advice. Can I go now?"

"Just one more thing. Where will you stay while your boat is healing?"

"I don't know," she said impatiently. "In town, I guess."

Alex shook his head, a vehemence he didn't know he possessed seeping into his blood. There was no way he was going to send this woman off to some hotel room. No matter how unwise, he wanted her close, where he could keep an eye on her, where he could protect her—where he could make certain she wouldn't leave Llandaron without his knowledge.

Not with the ominous possibility of his child growing inside her.

"You will stay here at my beach house."

Her brows shot together. "Just who do you think you are?"

"I told you who I am."

"Right. Future king. Right." She gestured around her. "I don't see any guards."

"I don't allow my guards in my private residence, nor are they allowed on the grounds."

"That's a little unsafe for the future king, isn't it?" she asked sarcastically.

"Perhaps. But after a lifetime of living 'beneath the shield of protection,' so to speak, it is what I have chosen."

She met his imperious gaze without flinching. "Look, buddy, what happened here was a mistake, okay? Can't we leave it at that? We weren't thinking. All that fog and having your life flash before your eyes can—"

"Can make one foolish?"

She pointed at him. "Exactly."

"Well, that doesn't stay the fact that you might be pregnant."

On a tiny gasp, her mouth dropped open and her gaze dropped to her belly. There was a long silence before her eyes finally met his once again. And when they did he saw pure unadulterated shock. Then, like a shifting breeze, anxiety and wonder filled those sea-green depths.

She said quietly, almost to herself, "Did you ever think that maybe I'm on the pill?"

"I don't think so."

"And why would you think that?" She lifted her

impish chin. "Am I so undesirable that I wouldn't have a steady boyfriend?"

Undesirable? Alex fairly chuckled at the thought. The word sounded like insanity coming from that full, sweet mouth he wanted to taste again. Just as the word *boyfriend* rang like an irritating bell in his brain.

His jaw tightened. He didn't want to think of her with another man, he didn't want to think of her taking birth control for an active love life. Both thoughts made his gut twist. But such feelings were dangerous.

"I wasn't meaning to insult you," he said tightly. "I just assumed… Well, you've been out to sea for at least four months. Alone. The need for companionship—"

She cut him off, her tone shaky, "How in the world could you know that I've been at sea for four months?"

"I saw you." The image of her standing on that boat, hair wild, all mind-numbing curves, slammed into his mind—along with the white-hot need that accompanied it.

"When?" she demanded. "When did you see me?"

"In Scotland. Back in May. I was on the beach. You were standing on the bow of your boat."

As the salty wind whipped around them, her eyes darkened to a rich green, pink stained her cheeks. "That was you?"

Alex nodded, his pulse jumping to life in his blood.

So she'd seen him, too.

Sophia knew her face was turning bright red in front of this man, and she hated herself for it. She wasn't one for embarrassment or awkward situations. In fact, she pretty much ran headfirst into conflicts so they could be resolved and done with. But around this gorgeous creature she wasn't herself. And the fact that she'd had dreams, even fantasies about seeing him, bare-chested and formidable, etched into Scotland's rocky coastline for a full month afterward, made her even more disheartened.

"Who are you? Really?" she asked him, tucking a strand of hair behind her ear.

"Crown Prince Alexander William Charles Octavos Thorne." The grin he gave her made her knees soft as cream. "Really."

"You're lying."

He shook his head. "I don't lie."

Breath held, she studied him in the light of the fading sun. Her grandfather had always said she was a great judge of character. But this man was harder to read than most. He seemed to have iron bars shooting up around him.

But even so, in those heather-colored eyes, in that solemn set of his jaw she saw honor—she saw truth.

She turned away, back toward the sea, with a groan. This was impossible. Impossible. Such things didn't happen in real life. A prince, for heaven's sake.

Had she really gone and done something so outrageous as to make love to a prince?

Her hand went to her stomach.

A child... An oh-so-familiar ache surged into her throat. She'd been an only child, treated as an adult with all the responsibilities that came with it since the age of five. Ever since, she'd dreamed about having a family, a brood of kids. Teaching them to read, to sail, to swim and, most important, to be silly and carefree—to be a kid.

But having a child this way...

And with royalty...

For a moment Sophia thought that maybe she'd fallen asleep on the deck of the sloop that afternoon. Under the hot sun. Maybe her mind had played tricks and this was all just one crazy dream. The crash, the fog, the man...

With a dash of hope in her heart, she reached over and pinched her arm. A sudden sting told her that she was very much awake.

"And your name?" he asked.

Sophia glanced up at him and muttered a bleak, "Sophia Dunhill from San Diego, California."

With a grim smile the prince took her hand. "Come back to my house, Sophia, dry off, then we'll have your boat rescued."

"Good God. Not another American," the king exclaimed.

Leaning back against the palace library's black-walnut mantel, Alex crossed his arms over his chest and watched his brother, Maxim, and his newly-pregnant sister, Cathy, turn to their American spouses and break out into laugher.

Ten minutes ago Alex had left his spunky little mermaid to her bathing. She'd sworn up and down that she would stay put "at least for tonight," she'd said. He didn't know whether to believe her or not, but what he did know was that if he hadn't taken a break from her presence, he would have pulled her into his arms and made love to her again.

Now, just the thought of her nude, in his bath, up to her neck in vanilla-scented suds…

His hands balled into fists under his crossed arms. Control had to return, must return.

"Unlike my brother and sister," Alex began with a frown. "There is no…romance here, father."

The king gave his regal wolfhound, Glinda, a pat on the head, then leaned back in his favorite armchair and took a swallow of brandy. "I should hope not. This would be a very unwise time to go running around with—"

"Some American, Your Highness?" Maxim's wife, Fran, said on a chuckle.

Alex watched as the king tried to jolt his pregnant and very American daughter-in-law with a withering look, but it came out as a lopsided grin instead. And when the pretty veterinarian returned the smile and patted him on the knee, the old man actually blushed.

The sight of his father turning from staunch dictator to blushing teddy bear stunned Alex. He'd never seen that side of his father. Not since he'd returned home, at any rate. It didn't take a masters in psychology to deduce that this "American" had done the softening up.

Maxim turned to Alex, grinned. "So, she turned up on the beach, did she?"

Alex nodded succinctly. He wasn't elaborating. The particulars of his encounter with Sophia on the beach didn't need to be shared. As it was, the truth wouldn't stop playing over and over in his mind; visions were more than enough. "Her boat needs extensive repairs."

"And you volunteered to put her up until it's fixed?" Cathy's husband, Dan, asked with a grin to match Maxim's. The new head of palace security was not only a former U.S. Marshal, but far too inquisitive for his own good.

Alex muttered tightly, "That's right. It was my stretch of beach she washed up on. I would say that holds me responsible."

Dan and Maxim exchanged wry glances.

"Didn't you used to dream about mermaids when you were little?" Cathy asked, taking a sip of her cranberry juice.

"He certainly did," Maxim said.

Fran smiled broadly and snuggled closer to her husband who had her very sleepy wolfhound pup, Lucky, on his lap. "How very romantic."

Dan turned to his wife. "So what were these dreams about, Angel?"

Alex sighed heavily. "When did these family dinners start?"

They all ignored him as Cathy explained, "Alex was always a stoic child. He rarely told us anything...private. But when he started having these dreams, the same one, every night for a full year, he couldn't keep it to himself. I was rather young, but I still remember how my big brother, my very stoic, grumbling brother, looked when he'd tell us about this dream."

"All right, that's enough," Alex said, his voice laced with warning.

Maxim chuckled. "Not nearly."

Cathy smiled and continued, "He would sit on the roof of the stables and look out at the ocean and tell us all about her. Long red hair, green eyes, pale skin stepping out of the sea with her arms outstretched."

"Don't forget about her magical powers," Maxim prompted.

Quite caught up in the whole mess, the king inquired, "What's this about magic?"

Dan and Fran nodded quickly, both inquiring, "What about her magical powers?"

Alex groaned, stalked over to the bar and filled a

glass with whiskey. How could such a stupid, adolescent dream come back to haunt him this way? And where were the silent and very sedate family dinners he'd always enjoyed—and had counted on tonight?

Cathy's words came out like a sigh. "He said that when she looked at him he felt as though he could fly, as though he was free, as though he could do and be anything."

Alex cursed, his knuckles white as he gripped the glass of whiskey.

Dan snorted. "What do you make of that, Max? Poetry or something?"

Maxim shrugged. "I'm not certain. But it sounds as though he was in love with her."

Alex glared at his brother and sister. "You know, there are plenty of humiliating stories I can share with your spouses."

Fran grinned widely, her eyes lighting up. "Oooo. Like what?"

Maxim gave his wife a kiss on the cheek. "He's bluffing, sweetheart."

"You want to try me, little brother?" Alex countered.

"How about after dinner," Fran suggested on a chuckle. "When we're all full and not as prickly." She turned to Alex. "So, what does this Sophia look like?"

Alex shook his head at his new sister-in-law. She was quick, very quick. Turning the conversation back to him and this mystery they all seemed to want to solve. He should be steaming mad. But no man could be angry with this woman for long—that was clear. Smart, beautiful and glowing with pregnancy.

He stilled, his mind returning to a beach house not far away. Would Sophia glow from carrying his child?

"Red hair by any chance?" Fran asked softly.

With a wave of the hand, Alex tossed out without thinking, "Red hair, green eyes and pale skin. Don't know about the magical powers."

Everyone fell silent, only the crackling of the fire and the subtle tinkling of ice cubes in glasses could be heard. Alex could fairly feel them gaping at each other over what he'd just said.

"Why would she not come to dinner tonight?" the king asked at last.

"She wanted some time to herself," Alex said tightly. "And after…the stress of losing her boat today, I thought it best not to overwhelm her." He didn't add *in her condition*—or potential condition.

The king drained his glass, then announced, "I would like to meet this young woman."

Cathy nodded. "I think we all would."

"How about a picnic lunch on the hill tomorrow?" Fran suggested. "With Aunt Fara and Ranen, and Glinda and the pups, too."

Chest tight, Alex stared at his family as they planned and plotted a way to meet his new houseguest. Everything was being taken out of his hands today. What happened at the beach with Sophia; his strange need for her. And now the insistence of his family. He felt as though he was just an onlooker, a bystander, in his own life. As though some force of nature had taken over.

But before Alex could even attempt to snatch back any semblance of control, his father stood up and barked his command. "Very good. A picnic on the hill. That's settled, then. Let's go in to dinner now."

Sophia stepped out of the bath feeling only mildly relaxed. Here she was, in the crown prince of Llandaron's opulent bathroom of pristine white and rugged navy, attempting to soak off the day's craziness.

But how could she soak away unease and hope, not to mention a need unlike any she'd ever felt before?

Her shrink back in San Diego would have a field day with her behavior today. Normally their sessions were comprised of past regrets and pains: her lonely childhood, her parents' death, her devotion to her beloved grandfather, her wariness to get involved with, then subsequently lose someone she loved.

But this…

This situation that she'd found herself in was beyond all analysis.

Sophia stepped over to the gold-encrusted mirror above the sink, dropped her towel and stared at her reflection. Bright eyes, pink lips, flushed cheeks. She had the look of a woman who'd experienced lust and excitement and satisfaction. The look of a woman who'd just had life breathed into her.

The double meaning in those words had Sophia touching her belly.

A soft smile moved through her. She and Alex had made love at a very risky time. But was such a miracle even possible? Could a life be growing inside her from a moment in time that was as wonderful as it was insane? And if so, what in the world was she going to do about it?

She lifted her chin, her gaze again to the mirror. She would do as she'd always done—face life head-on, face her fears and live each moment with no regrets.

No regrets.

"Sophia?"

Sophia gasped at the masculine call, reached down and snatched up her towel. Alex was back from dinner. Way too early. No doubt to check on her, make sure she hadn't run away.

With a quick shiver, Sophia glanced over her shoulder at the bathroom door. She swallowed hard. It stood open a good foot. He was right outside, and his close proximity made her feel as though she couldn't move, as though her feet were stuck to the bathroom tiles. "I didn't expect you back so soon. Could you close the door, please? I'll be out in a minute."

She heard him snort. "Don't tell me you've become shy all of a sudden."

"Not all of a sudden," she mumbled.

"Is that right? And today—"

"Today I was temporarily blinded by—"

"Lust?" he offered.

"More like a near-death experience. Now, are you going to close the door or what?"

"Not just yet. I'm rather intrigued by the 'or what.'"

On a frustrated sigh, and without thinking, she stalked to the doorway and faced him. "You are impossible!"

"And you are…"

"I'm impossible, too. Now, what can I do for you?"

His fierce gaze raked boldly over her. "You shouldn't ask a man such a question wearing only that scrap of cotton."

Sophia pulled her towel closer. "Are you telling me that I can't trust you to be a gentleman?"

"That's exactly what I'm telling you."

Heat moved through her, but she kept her tone cool. "Let's get one thing straight, sire. Today was a lapse in judgment. It's not going to happen again."

He nodded succinctly. "Fine."

"Fine?"

"I don't supplicate, Sophia."

"Good. And I don't kowtow to royalty."

His mouth twitched with amusement. "Just so we

understand each other...." He gestured behind him. "Now get dressed and come out. I brought you dinner."

She glanced past him, saw several steaming, silver chafing dishes on the glass dining table. "I appreciate the thought, Alex, but I'm not very hungry."

"You will eat, Sophia," he insisted with a vague hint of disapproval.

"Maybe you didn't hear me a moment ago, but I won't be commanded to do—"

"This isn't about you." A muscle twitched in his jaw, his eyes growing dark as eggplant. "You will not starve my child."

Sophia's body stiffened with shock, her mind reeling. Alex's words, his command, cut her deep, deeper than she could have imagined. Just the thought of harming a child, her child, a child that might be growing inside of her at this very moment, brought tears to her eyes.

She blinked them back and took a calming breath. "I'll be out in a minute."

He nodded, a hint of warmth passing over his dark and very dangerous gaze. But it was gone quickly. And after a moment he took a step back and closed the bathroom door.

# Three

---

Holding two mugs of coffee, one black as mud, the other creamy and decaffeinated, Alex followed Sophia out onto the beach house's sprawling deck. "What are you thinking so seriously about tonight?"

"My future."

"And what do you see?"

She shrugged. "It's very uncertain, isn't it?"

"I suppose it is," he said, sliding the mugs of steaming liquid onto the teak sombrero table.

All around them, the night sky gleamed clear, but for the brilliant clusters of stars winking down at them. A cool sea breeze blew across the beach, shifting specks of sand here and there.

Alex motioned for Sophia to take a seat at one of the rustic dining chairs, but she shook her head, then headed down the stairs. When she reached the bottom, she gave a weighty sigh and sat down on the last step, dug her toes in the sand.

"I'm not used to being on this side of the sand," she said. "But it's very beautiful."

Alex watched her stare out at the ocean as it crashed against the shore in cloudy tufts, biting his tongue from telling her just what *he* found beautiful on this side of the sand.

Instead he followed her down the stairs. "Why have you been sailing the isles for four months, Sophia?"

"I don't know if you'd understand the reason."

"Why?"

She glanced over her shoulder, gave him a half-smile. "You seem too, well…practical."

"You have the wrong perception of me," he said, dropping down beside her on the step.

"Wacky, wild and crazy, are you, your highness?"

"I can be." He glanced out toward the sand, the place where they'd made love not long ago. "Tell me about your journey," he said, trying to shove away the surge of desire that was running through him at a hectic pace.

Her voice softened. "Well my parents died when I was young, and I didn't think I had any family besides my horribly overbearing aunt. I was so afraid of her. She was so much like my parents. Too protective, too concerned, yet totally invulnerable." She released a sigh. "But then I found out that I had a grandfather."

She pulled her knees into her chest, smiled. "He came and got me. He took me in, raised me on his houseboat, taught me to embrace challenges instead of being afraid of them. We spent nearly every day on the water. The man was beyond wonderful. He treated me like I was special and loved. He made me smile every day that he was alive."

Alex had never heard someone speak in such a way. Open and honest with absolutely no pretense. He wasn't sure what to make of it. "When did your grandfather pass away?"

"Last year."

"I'm sorry, Sophia."

"Me, too. We were almost finished with the *Daydream*. His one wish in life was to sail the Isles."

Alex smiled with understanding. "You are doing this for him?"

"Yes," she said softly. "Llandaron is the last leg on my tour. But..."

"You didn't get all the way around her?"

She nodded.

He was schooled in the ways of diplomacy and tact, but comfort didn't come easy to him. He eased a wayward strand of red hair off her cheek and said, "You will."

Sophia turned to look at him. "I have to, Alex. Llandaron was very important to my grandfather. Especially Baratin. He was born there, lived there until he was thirteen."

Alex paused, shot her a glance of utter disbelief. "You have family here?"

She shook her head. "I don't think so. Not anymore, anyway. Gramps never spoke of family."

"Dunhill. That doesn't sound familiar to me."

"No it wouldn't. That was my father's name. My grandfather was my mother's father. He was taken away from Llandaron by his aunt when his mother died."

"What was your grandfather's name?"

"Turk. Robert Turk."

Shock slammed through Alex, rendering him temporarily speechless. Robbie Turk. He hadn't heard that name in years; to one of his clansmen it was the closest thing to blasphemy. But there was nothing for it now. The man's granddaughter had come home, and the man's family had a right to know.

With a thread of protective instinct fueling his blood, Alex snaked an arm around Sophia's waist. "Come back upstairs now and have your coffee. It's getting late."

Sophia stared wide-eyed at the scene before her. In America a picnic typically consisted of something like fried chicken, potato salad, strawberries, Jell-O mold and all the ants you could handle from within a five-block radius.

What was unfolding on the oh-so-picturesque bluff above Llandaron was no picnic. It was a fantasy, a royal affair, a scene from some Merchant Ivory film.

Not that the members of the royal family were wearing white lace and carrying parasols. Actually, they were casually dressed. Khaki and blue, a little lavender to match the heather growing wild around them. No, what made the picture so superb, what made a girl catch her breath, was the beautiful table setup, the elegant wait staff and the killer scenery.

Like a sentinel, the bluff sat quietly overlooking miles of ocean, only showing off its grassy cap to those who had the good fortune to climb it. Thickly rooted trees gave plenty of shade to the family and to the long teak table spread with fruit and meats, oysters and wine, cheeses and fresh bread.

"Don't worry." Alex took her hand and squeezed it. "They don't bite."

"I'm fine, Alex," she said with a confidence she really didn't feel.

"Nothing makes you tremble, right?"

"That's right."

To be honest, she really wanted to impress these people. Which was totally unlike her. Normally she couldn't give a whit what others thought of her—a trait passed down by her grandfather—royal or not. But the people that Alex was guiding her toward were his family, and she wanted them to like her. If she really was carrying his child, this group would be its family. And there was nothing she wanted more for her child than a loving family.

Alex led her into the center of the gathering. "I want to introduce you to my father first."

"The king?" she whispered.

"Yes." He raised an amused brow at her. "I thought you weren't afraid—"

"I'm not afraid. I just thought that maybe we'd start out with someone easier. Like a duke or a countess or something."

He chuckled, squeezed her hand again. "Come on."

The king of Llandaron sat on a large white arm-chair, legs apart, his countenance fierce and formidable. He was broad-shouldered and battle-scared. But the deep lines etched into his face were not from combat; more likely from years of negotiations and treaties. Whatever the reason for his powerful presence, when self-proclaimed brave soul Sophia stepped into his gaze, she actually felt her knees buckle a little.

"Your Majesty," Alex began. "This is Sophia Dunhill, Sophia, my father, King Oliver Thorne."

Sophia inclined her head as she'd seen many do in the movies and hoped it was appropriate here. "It's nice to meet you, Your Majesty."

The king looked her over. From the tips of the

brand-new sneakers she'd bought that morning to the new jeans and white peasant blouse that had accompanied them and up to her makeup free face and loose hair.

"Odds fish, Alexander," the man exclaimed. "She really does have the look of your mermaid about her, doesn't she?"

Caught completely off guard, Sophia fairly choked as she whirled to face her escort. "Your what?"

The king's hearty chuckle filled the air.

Alex's lips thinned. "It's nothing," he muttered, taking her hand again. "Thank you for that, Father."

"You are most welcome, my son."

"Let's find some shade, shall we?" Alex said dryly, leading her away.

Sophia managed another tilt of the head and a quick, "It was good to meet you, Your Majesty."

The king called merrily after them, "And you, my dear."

"Are you going to explain yourself, sire?" Sophia asked Alex as he led her toward the buffet table.

"After lunch."

"Fine. But I'll hold you to that."

"I'm sure you will.

Sophia grinned. "Listen, before we eat, I'd like to meet the rest of your family."

He sniffed proudly. "And after that bit of lunacy with my father there's nothing I'd like less."

But he led her over to a group of jovial men and

women, anyway, introduced her to each, then gave every last one of them the evil eye and stern instructions to keep all discussions of mermaids and past childhood apparitions out of the conversation.

As the group gave a not-so-convincing, yet collective, nod, Sophia made a mental note to ask Alex about the second part of his warning as well as the first.

But the inquisition would have to wait until after lunch she quickly realized as Alex, his handsome brother, Maxim, and rugged brother-in-law, Dan, were locked into a debate over football and the lack of quality players on this year's teams. This left Alex's violet-eyed sister, Cathy, and beautifully pregnant sister-in-law, Fran, with Sophia.

It was odd, but Sophia felt an immediate kinship with the two women. Fran was also from California, down-to-earth and welcoming. Cathy was nothing like the stuck-up princess Sophia had expected. She was incredibly kind and warm and strong willed. They were the girlfriends that she'd never had and always wished for, and the urge to spill her guts about what had happened between Alex and her was strong.

But she was a wary creature by nature and kept what had happened yesterday where it belonged: in the fog.

"So, you came here to care for the king's wolfhound?" Sophia asked Fran.

The pretty blonde pointed to the sleeping dog behind the king's chair. "Glinda had a brood of beautiful pups." She stroked the head of the large puppy at her feet. "If you can believe it, Lucky here was the runt."

"You got to keep one of her pups? How wonderful."

Fran smiled broadly. "Got a pup, a prince and a baby out of the deal."

Cathy laughed. "Plus a sister and a pain-in-the-neck brother-in-law."

"Don't say that," Fran warned in good humor, touching her burgeoning belly. "His child can hear you."

"Oh, Lord, and so can mine."

The women laughed and rubbed their stomachs. For some stupid reason, so did Sophia.

Fran saw her and frowned. "Are you okay?"

Blushing, Sophia quickly dropped her hand from her flat belly and smiled. "Fine. Just...hungry." She stood up. "Can I get either of you something?"

"Maybe just some biscuits and cheese," Fran said, and Cathy nodded.

Sophia headed for the buffet, calling herself all kinds of idiot. She didn't need to get attached here— to the people, to the land, to Alex and even to a child she wasn't sure she was carrying.

Maybe after lunch she'd head over to the boat works, see how the *Daydream* was faring and get her mind on the realties of her life.

"Sophia," she heard Alex call from behind her.

When Sophia turned, Alex, an older couple and another wolfhound pup were all walking toward her. A strange palpitation started in her blood, fast and uneasy as she stared at the wrinkled old man beside Alex. His eyes—strangely memorable eyes—fairly bored a hole in her heart as around them the sea released a salty breath.

"There are two people I haven't introduced you to, Sophia." Alex grinned. "They have just now arrived. I think you'll find this introduction fascinating."

The thin, exquisitely beautiful older woman took Sophia's hand, her violet eyes warm and inviting. "My name is Fara."

"My aunt," Alex supplied.

Sophia smiled, feeling incredibly tentative and not knowing the reason for it. "How nice to meet you, Your Highness."

"And you, Sophia."

Alex's aunt was terribly sweet and welcoming, but Sophia's focus was all for the frowning man, weathered and worn, at the woman's side.

If this had been a dream, Sophia would have reached out for him for he looked so familiar. Or maybe he felt familiar…she wasn't sure.

"And who might you be, lass?" the man uttered, his voice gravel-like and thick with that husky Llandaron burr.

"My name is Sophia Dunhill." She couldn't stop herself from asking, "Who are you, sir?"

He stuck out his gnarled hand. "The name's Ranen. Ranen Turk."

Sophia mouth dropped. So did her heart. She stood there, blank, amazed, shaken. "What did you say?"

"Just my name, lass."

"Turk?"

"Aye."

"Sophia?" Alex said, clearly concerned.

Fara put a hand on her shoulder. "Are you all right, my dear?"

But Sophia barely heard either one of them. Waves of utter disbelief were threatening to capsize her mind. "Did you know a Robert Turk from Baratin?"

The man's face turned instantly sour as he ground out, "Don't speak that name to me, lass."

"Did you know him?"

Ranen scowled, his nostrils flaring. "My younger brother, he is. Deserted his family. A bloody bastard, he is."

"Ranen, please," Alex said sharply as his arm eased around Sophia's waist.

She leaned into his hold. "I don't understand."

"How do you know Robert?" Fara asked, caught somewhere between her concern for Ranen and her interest in Sophia.

Sophia couldn't take her eyes off Ranen. "He's...he's my grandfather."

Ranen's eyes widened to saucers, but he said nothing. For a good thirty seconds, the only sounds that could be heard were the rush of ocean to shore and the distant chatter of the picnickers.

Sophia fought for the right thing to say, the right questions to ask.

But she ran out of time. For after a moment Ranen turned on his heel and walked away.

The fax in front of him blurred.

Alex tossed the offending paper onto his cluttered desk, slung his head back and sighed. He had no mind for work right now. Four hours ago, he and Sophia had returned home from the picnic. Conversation had been tight and sparse. She'd looked pale and confused and had gone to her room almost immediately upon entering the house.

He'd wanted to comfort her, wanted to explain why he'd chosen to surprise her with Ranen's existence today, but he was inexperienced with apologies. Especially ones regarding a personal mistake.

Yet he couldn't just sit here and do nothing.

Dismissing the work on his desk, Alex left his office and went downstairs. The house was quiet, save for the muffled sound of the ocean. About thirty minutes ago, Sophia had emerged from her bedroom, towel in hand. She was going for a swim, she'd informed him soberly. The fog had receded, and she would stay close to shore.

That promise had done little to appease him, but he knew she needed the exercise. He knew she needed the comfort of the sea. He'd felt such a need many times himself.

Alex breathed in the salty air the moment he stepped outside his front door and onto the deck. Twilight had painted the canvas of sky a magnificent violet. But he didn't give the scenery more than a glance. He wanted to find her, had to find her.

As promised, she was swimming close to shore, taking the easy waves with natural grace. Alex watched as she dove under the water, then emerged, her hair slicked back, profile stunning, shoulders soft and wet. She made one drop-dead silhouette, and he couldn't stop himself from recognizing that it was the perfect recreation of his childhood dream.

Nor could he stop himself from going to her. Under the Van Gogh sky, he jogged toward the water's edge, stripped off his shirt and shorts. He tried to tell himself that a quick dip would bring back his sanity. When he dove beneath the waves, he told himself that the cool water would heal him.

But when he found himself face-to-face with her, standing inches away in belly-deep water, he had to admit that he was a fraud.

The truth was, he wanted to be near her. Just like the ginger-haired mermaid in his dream, when he was around Sophia he felt alive and free.

"Pretty brave of you, Highness," she said, wiping away the droplets of water streaming down her face.

"Why is that?"

"Returning to the scene of the crime—aka, the near-death experience."

"Well, you saved me once. I expect you'd do it again if the need arises."

"I don't know. Look what kind of trouble that brought last time."

A wave pelted them both, sending them sideways a foot. "You'd let me drown just to protect yourself against—"

"Pain?" she offered, smiling.

"I was thinking pleasure."

She shook her head. "We're not going there again, Alex."

If only that were true, Alex mused. If only they possessed that level of control. He was willing to bet his life that neither one of them did. But he offered her a flippant "Anything you say, Sophia," anyway.

She wasn't buying. "You say that as if you fully expect me to cave."

"Cave?"

"Like you expect me—at some point, when I can't stand it anymore—to reach out, grab you and haul you against me."

His chest tightened, as did the rest of him. "Perhaps there's no expectation. Perhaps there's only curiosity and…hope."

He saw her lips part, saw her tongue dart out and swipe her bottom lip. Then felt his own reaction, deep in his groin.

"I'm curious," he continued, his pulse jolting in his blood. "What would happen after you hauled me against you?"

"I don't know," she murmured silkily. "I'd kiss you, I suppose."

"Hard or soft?"

Her eyes darkened to a deep green. "Maybe both."

"What then?"

"I don't know."

"Yes you do." He moved closer but didn't touch her. "Would you wrap your legs around my waist?"

"Probably."

Alex could hardly contain himself. He was ready to pounce. His hands were balled into fists under the water, his groin painfully tight. But he fought for control. This had to come from her.

"Sounds nice, Sophia, but—"

"But?" she uttered incredulously. "But what?"

"It's a pretty bold move."

"And you don't think I'm bold?"

He grinned, moved closer, within inches. "No."

Her brows snapped together as the wind whipped her wet hair about her body. "Excuse me?"

"I'm just saying that taking what you want without the protection of the fog and with no excuses is—"

"You don't think I'm up to it?"

Alex didn't have a chance to answer. He was being thrust forward, long, toned legs wrapping his waist, beautiful, moist mouth closing in on his.

And he took, wanting all she could give.

His hands raked up her thighs until he found her sweet backside. He gripped her tightly, squeezing, feeling her curves as around them night fell and ocean quaked. She made a soft whimpering sound, and Alex took her tongue into his mouth, holding his ground, digging his feet into the sand to keep them upright.

She tasted of saltwater and heaven, pure perfection. He held her tighter, possessively. She was his. Right now at any rate, right now, she belonged to him.

They twisted and struggled as they kissed like long-lost lovers eager to learn each other's taste and scent once again. Until Sophia broke the spell, broke the kiss and raised her head.

"Have I proved myself, Your Highness?"

Jaw as tight as the rest of him, Alex released her. "You are very bold, Sophia."

She nodded, her breathing still labored. "I'm going in now. You coming?"

"In a minute."

She turned away, waded into shore, then stopped and turned back. "You'll be all right out here by yourself?"

"I always have. I always will."

He saw her flinch slightly before saying, "Good night, then."

Alex watched her go, all the way up the sandy beach and into the house. When she was safely inside, he turned and dove into a wave. His mind was blistered from their silly game, and his groin screamed with pain.

But it wasn't merely madness and unrequited pleasure that plagued him. Those two shackles he could deal with, had for his entire marriage—as he was no rogue, no cheating husband.

No, it was something far more dangerous.

For the first time in six years, he felt connected with life—open to lust, to need, to pain and to want.

And Sophia Dunhill was his keeper of the keys....

# Four

***

*Sara Squirrel hugged the acorn close to her chest
and smiled....*

Her back to a small beach rock, Sophia sighed into
the ocean breeze, scribbled over the rotten sentence
and started again.

*When Sara Squirrel woke up that morning she just
knew that today was the day she was going to find
her family....*

A moderately satisfied smile curved Sophia's
mouth. Better. Not great. But better than the last attempt.

Was it possible? she wondered, fiddling with her
finely sharpened pencil. Could the wild lushness of

Llandaron be causing the dense walls of her brain to come tumbling down? Or was it the allure, the kisses of a tall, dark and very handsome prince?

The blush of a silly teenager with a crush on her heart crept into Sophia's cheeks. With a snort, she shut her notebook and dropped back against the stone. It had been one week since she'd jumped ship and come to shore. One week since she'd made love to Alex. And in that week, she'd rarely thought of anything but him—those probing eyes, those crushing lips on hers and, of course, the amazing possibility that they'd made a child together.

Life would've been much easier if the pull she felt for him was nothing more than physical. But it wasn't. The way he challenged her, made her think and wonder about things she'd never contemplated before—they all conspired against her, making her desire for him as a partner, as well as a lover, intense and undeniable.

And she, who only wanted freedom. She who never needed anyone.

Or thought she didn't.

Sophia stared out at the sea, watched the heavy waves curl into a peak and crash to shore. She shivered with the weight of their descent.

"Been avoiding us, have you? Or is it just me?"

Sophia whirled around, startled. Standing above her on the rock was Ranen. At his feet, sat the panting wolfhound pup with wide, sweet brown eyes she'd seen with him at the picnic.

"Jeez," she said with a breathless laugh. "You scared the life out of me."

"Sorry about that." With the agility of a man half his age, Ranen jumped down from the rock. The pup followed suit. "In fact, I'm right sorry about a couple things. But you won't make me name them all, will you, lass?"

Her heart warmed at his words, vague though they were. "Of course not." She understood his pride as she'd understood her grandfather's.

"So, have you seen anything besides His Highness's beach house in the last week?" he asked quickly.

"I went down to the boat works this morning, as a matter of fact."

"How long before your rig is back afloat?"

"Two weeks."

He nodded, quick and tight—and familiar. He was so much like her grandfather it almost ached to look at him. Yet it was strangely comforting, too. This man who was all the family she had left and was too angry, too stubborn to recognize it.

As though offering her comfort, the brown-eyed wolfhound pup sidled up to her and lay down. Warmth spread from the pup's body to Sophia in seconds, soothing her senses, calming her heart.

"Her name is Aggie," Ranen said, leaning against the rock.

"She's lovely."

"Follows me everywhere, she does. A regular pain in the arse."

Sophia chuckled as she stroked the pup's wiry fur and said without thinking, "My grandfather used to say the same thing about our cat, Smoke. But if that cat wasn't on his lap purring at least three hours a night, Gramps was totally out of sorts."

It was little surprise that Ranen chose not to respond. Instead he pointed to her notebook. "What are you working on there?"

"A new story. Hopefully." She shrugged, explained, "I'm a writer. Children's books. And I'm desperately trying to stomp out some writer's block."

"Sounds pretty serious."

"It can be if it goes on long enough. And I've had the problem ever since…"

She paused, sat uneasily in the sand.

"Since when?" Ranen probed.

"Since my grandfather died."

Sudden anger lit the old man's eyes. He cleared his throat. "So the old bugger passed on, did he?"

Sophia nodded, her throat tight with feeling. "Last year."

With a tight jaw, Ranen dropped down beside her on the sand. He was silent as he stared toward the ocean. Sophia so desperately wanted to ask him about her grandfather's life in Baratin and why there was a rift between them, why they'd never spoken in all those many years.

But she didn't get the chance when Ranen offered, "My grandmother was a writer."

"Really?" Her voice rose in surprise.

"Poetry."

"I'd love to read some."

He shrugged. "Perhaps I'll give you a few to look over. If I can find 'em, you understand."

"Oh, that would be wonderful, Ranen."

"Tosh," he grumbled. "Perhaps I could take you by the house today. But first, Aggie and I are going to the Llandaron Picnic. It's a yearly gathering. Whole town'll be there. And since you're here in town, you must come along with us."

Just the thought of going to a town function made her feel weary and unsure of herself. She didn't know her place here—if she had a place here. And she sure wasn't prepared to answer questions about Alex and her if they arose. "I'd like to, Ranen. Really I would. But I have so much work—"

"This isn't an invitation, lass. But orders from the king." He stood, brushed the sand from his already dusty pants. "Crown Prince Alexander is speaking, and he's going to be needing all of our support."

"Support? For what?"

Two bristly brows shot together. "He hasn't told you?"

Sophia shook her head.

"Four months ago, the prince and his wife divorced. Now he must explain the situation to his people and hope that they accept him without a princess, without an heir."

A bundle of nerves rustled in Sophia's belly—exactly where a child might be, an heir might be. "Why wouldn't they accept him?"

"'Tis the way things have been for ages, lass. No man has become king without a wife. No man has remained king without an heir."

Nerves turned into strong stabs of fear. No wonder Alex had reacted so strongly, so intensely to the possibility of her being pregnant. "And Alex wants to be king."

A look of unwavering seriousness suffused his features. "More than anything."

And if she was carrying his child...

Sophia closed her eyes for a moment and tried to slow her racing pulse. But it was no use. If she were pregnant, her child would belong to Llandaron.

And therefore so would she.

*Apprehension has no place here.*

Alex drummed the words into his mind. And he knew that, if need be, he would repeat them until they became reality.

In all his thirty-five years, he'd never been fearful of standing up in front of his people. But today so much was at stake. His future, the one he'd grown up to expect, could be coming to an end. This is, if his people rejected him in favor of his brother. And in all honesty, they wouldn't be wrong in doing so. Every king to sit on the throne of Llandaron had preached the same edict: country, order and peace were secured by tradition and law.

And for Alexander Thorne, he would respect that directive and abide by the wishes of his people.

The stone steps leading up to the podium were long and heavy, but he managed them. And under a cloudless blue sky, he turned to face his people. Rows upon rows of interested faces staring up at him, waiting. No doubt they expected a greeting, a royal order to enjoy the picnic and the day, not an update of his marital status.

For a split second Alex thought his voice had gone, his will, too. But when he noticed a cloud of red hair and an infectious smile gazing up at him from the crowd, the tension inside him eased.

A reaction he never would have expected.

He'd made specific instructions that she shouldn't be told about the event. He didn't want her to hear about his failure. He didn't want her to see his people reject him.

With her, he felt a supreme amount of pride. Whether it was wise or not, her opinion mattered to him.

But there was nothing for it now.

With a nod to his people, he began....

Sophia eased back against the cool leather seats of the limousine. She'd never ridden in such luxury, and she rather liked it. Outside the tinted windows, the quaint town shuffled by at a leisurely pace as the driver made his way toward the beach.

Beside her, Crown Prince Alex sat in regal silence. No doubt reviewing his performance this afternoon.

"I have always been ready to give my life for my country," he'd said. "Today, I give my heart, my soul and my future."

A slow shiver inched its way up Sophia's spine. A man with impassioned words and an unselfish nature made a woman's—well, made this woman's—knees weak.

Sophia ventured a glance in his direction. Stubborn jaw, aquiline nose, fiery violet eyes beneath thick black brows. Yes, he was something to behold, both in looks and in character.

She let her breath ease out of her lungs as she tried to calm her racing pulse. Never in her life had she wanted to jump into a man's lap, kiss him senseless, feel that rush of heat in her belly as he returned her ardor, his fingers threading in her hair.

There was no doubt about it. She was in trouble. For not only had Alex Thorne won over his country's heart today, he'd taken Sophia's right along with it. A heart she'd always thought an impassive muscle when it came to romance. A take-it-or-leave-it sort of thing.

But with Alex, she wanted to take.

"Are you all right?"

Sophia turned at Alex's query, nodded. "Fine. How about you? After a day like that I'm betting you're pretty keyed up."

He grinned in his way; that confident quirk of the mouth. "It went well."

"I would say so."

"I'm glad you came, Sophia."

"So am I. You were really wonderful."

He snorted, shifted back against the seat. "I was laid bare."

"Well, no man ever looked so good naked."

She sucked in a breath, her words echoing in her ears. For someone who was trying to play it cool, she was failing miserably.

Further proof positive was Alex's killer grin and husky, "Thank you, Sophia."

"Don't get cocky, your highness," she said with mock reproach. "You know what I mean."

He sighed heavily. "Yes, but I wish I didn't."

She couldn't help but laugh. "We get in trouble together, did you ever notice that? Verbally and otherwise?"

"Otherwise," he lamented. "Ah, yes, I miss otherwise."

Chuckling, she gave him a playful swat on the arm.

"You know, Highness, since you've been laid bare today—as you put it—maybe you can come completely clean."

"What do you have in mind?"

"Maybe now you can finally tell me about this mermaid business your father mentioned."

His smile faded. "I'd rather not."

"You did promise."

"Yes, I did." He waved an impatient hand. "All right, here it is then. When I was a boy I had a dream...several dreams, in fact...about the ocean and a certain..."

"A certain what?" she pressed eagerly.

"Mermaid coming out of the water," he ground out.

A slow smile eased its way to Sophia's lips. "The king said that I look like this mermaid?"

Through gritted teeth, he muttered, "Yes."

"Is it my hair?"

"Among other things."

"Like what?" she asked, batting her eyelashes.

He chuckled halfheartedly. "You're a tease."

"And you're much too far away."

His left eyebrow rose a fraction. "Excuse me?"

Groaning, she said, "I told you we get into trouble verbally and—"

She never got to finish that sentence as Alex reached out and dragged her to him. For just a quick second, as she stared up into violet desire, Sophia thought about doing what she'd only fantasized about doing: hurling herself into Alex's lap, wrapping her arms around his neck and kissing him senseless. But if she started this again, where would it end? What if she weren't pregnant and had to leave? And what if she was and this was only a physical connection. After all, he'd just gotten out of a relationship and it was perfectly clear he wasn't interested in another. Was she willing to risk her heart on an affair?

Alex brushed his thumb over her bottom lip. "If you want to kiss me, Sophia, all you have to do is tip that chin up and close your eyes and I'd be happy to oblige."

"You are way too full of yourself, you know that?"

Alex lowered his head, kissed her softly on the lips. When he pulled back it was only an inch. "I'd like to be full of you."

His kiss sent swirling currents of heat into her belly. He was so persuasive with just a look, a glance, a touch. She knew she was staring longingly at him, willing him to just take her without discussion so she didn't have to think or give in.

"Alex—"

"Yes, lass?"

Sophia melted at the husky, lusty burr, glanced toward the partition where the driver was in full view. "Are we close to home?"

"Ten minutes or so."

"Ten whole minutes?"

He chuckled softly, then reached over the side panel and grabbed an iced bowl of fruit. "Here, let's both have a strawberry. Keep our mouths occupied."

As he held one to her mouth, heat shimmied down her belly, pooling low. She didn't want berries, dammit! Couldn't he see that she wanted kisses, only his kisses?

Why wasn't she acting the way she had that first day on the beach? Taking what she wanted with no fear?

No answers came as Alex rubbed the berry between her lips with gentle insistence. She could feel his eyes on her as she opened her mouth, let him slip the fruit between her teeth.

When she bit down juice splattered all over her chin.

She grinned. "You planned that."

"Do you think I'm that powerful, Sophia?" he asked, gaze sliding downward. "That I can command a strawberry to burst? For sweet, pink juice to dribble down your chin and onto your blouse?"

"Yes." She looked down at the droplets of juice winding a path down, down, toward the valley between her breasts. "My blouse..."

"Let me get that."

"Do you have a towel or napkin or something?"

"No, I don't think so." Alex reached up, depressed

a button on the ceiling. Up went the privacy window. "But I have an idea."

Sophia held her breath as his fingers brushed the top of her shirt. But before he unfastened a button, he glanced up. "Do you mind?"

Refusing to think, rationalize or wonder, she shook her head. Alex grinned and moved in, had three buttons unhooked in a breath. Sophia's heart jolted as little by little cool air met her heated skin.

"Sophia…" Alex lowered his head and brushed a kiss over the inner curve of her left breast. "You taste so sweet, Sophia."

"It's the strawberry juice," she said breathlessly.

"No, it's you."

With skillful fingers, he eased aside the lace cup of her bra, then nuzzled his way to her nipple, hard and aching. Sophia arched her back, silently begging him to taste, to tease. And he did. He took, just as she had been so unable to do a moment before. He took for both of them, and she was thankful.

A fire roared to life within her, like a wild creature set to run from its trap. And if it lost a limb, lost its heart, so be it.

Or lost its mind, she mused as Alex cupped her breast in his palm and took her swollen nipple into his mouth.

Sophia couldn't control the moan of pleasure that ripped from her throat. She didn't even try. And the unfettered sound spurred Alex on. His suckling became intense, almost rough as his free hand dropped to her belly, inched lower to the apex of her thighs. Sophia bucked against his palm. Alex pressed harder.

Then a dose of reality slashed into their little dream world as the limousine came to a halt.

"We've stopped," Sophia whispered, her breathing ragged.

"Aye." The word came out as a growl.

"I suppose this means we should, too."

On a curse, Alex lifted his head, then his gaze. "I want to know you inside and out, Sophia."

"We already know each other that way—"

"No." He cupped her face gently. "Not as I imagine. Not fast and furious. I want to take you slow and sweaty and—"

She shook her head. "Don't say any more." Slow meant thinking. Slow meant wondering about the future, hoping for more than she had a right to. *That* she didn't want.

Alex sat up, fell back against the seat. "All right. I won't say any more. For now. For today. For tonight."

To his right, the limousine door opened. But before he got out, he shot her a wickedly serious stare. "But I can't control this…whatever is happening here…for much longer."

On legs filled with water, Sophia followed him out of the car and into the house. She could still feel his kisses on her tight, aching skin, hear his soft burr echoing in her ears.

*I can't control this for much longer.*

Neither could she. Lord, neither could she.

# Five

―――

"This is a right of passage," Fran announced as she and Cathy escorted Sophia through the green doors of Gershins Taffy Shop with such reverence one would think they were entering a great cathedral instead of...

"A candy shop?" Sophia said, glancing around at all the brightly packaged offerings.

"It's not just candy," Fran counseled sagely. "It's more like a little piece of heaven."

"Mana from heaven?" Sophia teased with a hint of a smile.

Cathy tossed Fran a pitying look. "She's been so deprived."

Fran nodded her agreement. "She just hasn't tasted it yet. Once she does, she'll understand."

Following her new friends down a thin aisle lined with barrels of sweet-smelling confection, Sophia couldn't help but laugh. "Are you guys trying to tell me that this is some kind of magical taffy?"

Cathy snorted, snatched up a piece of rich caramel-colored taffy from a nearby barrel and thrust it to her. "Just remember, skeptics rarely get seconds."

Sophia laughed again as she took the candy and unwrapped it. She was having way too much fun with these women. A relatively new experience for her.

As a writer, she worked at home and had little social life, so friends were few and far between. Even as a child, she'd led a pretty isolated life on her grandfather's houseboat. An existence that had actually suited her well. For she felt welcomed and cared for there as she hadn't anywhere else. And that was proved when she started going to school. During the day, she would do her work, eat her lunch with a few of the quiet girls, but when that bell rang at the end of the day, she was out of there—back to the place she finally felt was home.

She honestly never thought she'd feel welcomed and cared about again. But around Fran and Cathy she did. So when they'd come by the beach house an hour ago and asked her to join them in town, she'd jumped at the chance.

Sophia paused, her mind quickly turning to mush

as she bit into that piece of chocolate taffy insanity that Cathy had given her. The muffled word, ''Ohmigod!'' slipped from her sugar-sweetened lips, followed by, ''This is...''

''I know!'' Cathy exclaimed with a huge grin, unwrapping a smallish tube of green-apple taffy.

''It's...it's like...'' Sophia stumbled with her words, with an accurate description for the cream and chocolate and salty sweetness exploding in her mouth.

Fran put a hand on her shoulder. ''We did warn you.''

Sophia shook her head. ''Seriously, I've never tasted anything like this. It must be the saltwater around here or—''

''Don't try and figure it out,'' Fran advised.

Cathy nodded. ''No, don't. It's just like a man.''

Fran's gentle laughter rippled through the air. ''I can't wait to hear this.''

''Don't try and figure a man out,'' Cathy said, unwrapping her second piece of apple taffy. ''Just sit back and enjoy the moment.''

''Oh, that's good.'' Fran popped the piece of root beer taffy she was holding into her mouth. ''That's very good.''

But Sophia was having a little trouble with the analogy. Images of Alex and her flickered like firelight against the back of her mind. Kisses and sweet caresses. Amethyst eyes probing her very soul. Words of desire and true fulfillment whispered in her ear.

How could she just enjoy the moment? Alex was like the taffy that sat temptingly all about her. She would always want more. She could so easily become addicted.

Fran nudged Cathy with her elbow. "I think we might've said the wrong thing."

"Or the right thing," Cathy said. "Let's see—men, taffy, enjoying the moment, a dreamy-eyed, pink-cheeked girl."

Fran grinned. "I see where you're going with this."

Coming out of her haze, Sophia looked from one smiling woman to the other. "I sure don't."

"Are you falling for my brother?" Cathy asked plainly.

Sophia fairly choked, but she managed to utter the word, "What?"

"I know he's a handful—"

"That's just what Max says, too," Fran tossed in.

Cathy continued, "But he is also brilliant, generous, kind—"

"You guys—"

"Funny, protective and—"

"Incredibly sexy?" Sophia said wryly.

Fran and Cathy paused, stared at Sophia. Then two matching grins turned to bubbling laughter. Hands on hips, Sophia tried to look staid, but it didn't take. After a moment she was laughing right along with them.

Cathy looped an arm through Sophia's, grabbed a sack of assorted taffy and started for the cash register. "She's one of us, that's for sure."

Sophia pointed to the bulging candy bag. "You are going to be sharing that, right?"

"Yep. Definitely one of us," Fran said, snatching up a handful of chocolate fudge taffy and following them.

The headline of the London newspaper stared back at Alex with raw, black eyes.

Former Wife of the Crown Prince of Llandaron Marries President of Garrison Bank. Couple Expecting First Child in May of Next Year.

The words seeped into Alex's blood, making his pulse pound a hostile rhythm. Why was he so angry over a story about a woman he never loved, having a child he was never meant to have?

No doubt, because the waves of failure had ebbed for a little while and now they were back full force.

No, it wasn't his ex-wife or her child that made him see red—it was himself, his own inadequacies and the questions that would never retreat: was he capable of making a woman happy? And if so, did he even want to attempt such a feat?

His mermaid drifted through his mind.

Yes, with her he wanted to. But was it because she might be carrying his child? Or was it more?

Did he want an heir so desperately he was willing to risk his soul again?

Alex leaned back in his chair, the answer to his silent query coming fast, almost viciously.

Never.

It was 6:00 a.m. on the following Saturday morning when Sophia knew that her life had changed forever.

One hour ago she'd woken up with a strange pang of nausea. Groggy, she'd slipped out of her bed and into the bathroom where she'd immediately thrown up.

At first, lying against the cool tiles, she'd wondered what she'd eaten the night before to warrant such a reaction. After all, she'd always had what her grandfather referred to as a cast-iron stomach. Steak, mashed potatoes and a pot of hot chocolate…nothing too dangerous.

Then, like a wrecking ball to a sturdy building, a thought had slammed into her foggy brain. A strangely soothing thought.

Lord, she mused now as she leaned back against the tub, could she really be—

"Sophia?" The call startled her, made her breath catch, and was followed by a knock at the door. "Are you all right?"

"Yes, fine," she answered quickly.

No doubt too quickly, for Alex sounded a tad uneasy when he asked, "Can I come in?"

Her pulse jumping to life in her blood, Sophia actually shook her head at the closed door. She wasn't ready for this, for him. Not yet. Not until she knew for certain.

"I'm okay, Alex," she said firmly. "Really. Go back to bed."

He chose not to hear her. The door squeaked open a crack and he peeked in, his eyes filled with concern. "What's wrong?"

Coming to her feet, Sophia said, "Nothing," then turned the faucet to cold and grabbed for her toothbrush.

Seeing him, his face, made everything seem different. As insane as it might be, she wanted to tell him that she might very well be carrying his child. She wanted him to wrap his arms around her and kiss her, joy illuminating his handsome face.

But what if there was only an expression of moderate pleasure and he never moved from his spot by the door—no hugs, no touching.

He would love the child, but never the child's mother.

"You look as pale as a sheet," Alex said, moving closer to her.

"I'm okay. I'm feeling much better now."

Again, he paid her assurances of "fineness" absolutely no attention. Instead, he snatched a washcloth off the towel rack and held it under the running water.

"What are you doing?" Sophia asked.

"Just stop talking and sit down."

"Alex, this really isn't necessary—"

"Why don't you let me decide that. Trust me, all right?"

That soft grin he tossed her way disarmed her, made her cast off any feelings of apprehension about the word *trust*, the two of them and their future.

She returned his smile. "Okay, Alex."

He took the toothbrush from her hand with gentle insistence and deposited it on the counter. Then with true tenderness, he eased her down on the lid of the toilet and began to wipe her face.

The cool cloth felt delicious against Sophia's heated skin, and she let her eyes drift closed. "That feels nice."

"What did I tell you? I bring no pain, only pleasure."

"Promise?"

Sophia felt the washcloth move over her mouth, then heard Alex say, "I will do my very best, lass."

"I know you will."

Silence took the room as Alex continued his ministrations. Fresh, cool water on her forehead, cheeks and neck. Sophia was almost asleep with he asked, "Did you have pizza again with Fran and Cathy last night?"

"Nope. Steak and potatoes."

"Perhaps there was a spice in the potatoes that didn't agree with you."

"Possibly."

"Or perhaps you're getting sick."

"Sick?" she mumbled.

"The flu."

"I don't think so, Highness."

There was a slow silence, then, "Sophia?"

"Hmmmm?"

"Open your eyes."

In her dreamy state, she did as he commanded. But once she saw him, saw the look in his eyes, she wished she hadn't.

Eyes a vivid violet, lips thinned, jaw tight as a trap, his words came out as a growl. "All I ask is that you tell me the truth."

Her stomach clenched tight. "I don't understand what you mean."

"Yes, I think you do." He stood up, dropped the cloth in the sink.

"Alex—"

"Just the truth, Sophia." Something fragile, almost desperate flickered in his eyes. "Please."

"I don't know the truth."

"What does that mean?"

This was going too fast. She wasn't prepared to say anything now. Foolish what-ifs sliced through her brain at a mile a minute. Why couldn't he have just stayed in bed? Why couldn't she have gotten sick after he'd left?

"Sophia?"

"This could be the spices in the potatoes, this could be stress, this could be the flu."

"Dammit, Sophia, talk to me."

Her heart was thumping so madly she was sure he could hear it. "And this could be a child."

"Dear God."

"I'm late. Two days."

# Six

Later that day, Alex stood outside the bathroom door, fighting the urge to pace. He had always prided himself on being a cool, calm and exceedingly rational person. But right now, he was so far removed from any of those three traits he barely recognized himself. For behind the bathroom door, his future was being decided.

Or perhaps it had been decided the moment he'd seen Sophia standing atop the deck of her grandfather's sloop four months ago.

Alex plowed a hand through his hair. He'd wanted a child for so many years, the actual possibility of such a dream seeing the light of day filled him with a desperation he hadn't known he possessed.

Yet, if Sophia was carrying his child, what did that mean? What was their future? No matter what the situation or how needful he felt for the woman, he had no intention of giving himself to anyone ever again. That much of his future was already decided.

He turned to the door once again, raised his fist to knock, then dropped it.

Bloody torture.

Was it too early for a drink? He glanced at his watch. Eleven o'clock in the morning.

Quite probably.

"Alex?"

Alex's head came up with a snap just as the door opened. Sophia emerged from the bathroom, face pale, lips thin. He searched her eyes for some sign, an answer. But he couldn't read her.

She managed a tremulous smile and a noncommittal "Hi."

Here they stood in the brightly lit hallway of his beach house, neither of them comfortable, neither prepared for what was about to be discussed. And all that Alex was capable of was a nod.

She took a deep breath. "I took the test."

"Sophia, you're killing me here," Alex practically growled, his chest tight, tense.

"You don't have to worry."

"What the hell does that mean?"

"Just that you have no extra burdens."

"Burdens?" he exclaimed, leaning back and giving

an impatient sigh. "I never said that having a child would be a—"

Nervously Sophia ran a hand through her hair. "You didn't have to, Alex. I know what you've been through with your ex-wife."

"What does that have to do with anything?"

"Just that your marriage was a difficult one. Five years is a long time to..." She touched his arm. "You've made it perfectly clear how much you're enjoying your freedom."

"This isn't about freedom from a child, Sophia."

She let her hand drop to her side, her tone running cool. "It's about freedom from women."

Alex didn't agree or disagree. He wasn't interested in a therapy session or rehashing a past that was past. He only wanted answers. And he usually got what he wanted.

"The test was negative?" he said, jaw tightening as his past rose up to clip him on the cheek. "Is that what you're saying?"

For a moment she only stared at him, her eyes guarded. Then she said softly, "Yes."

Alex had expected to feel at least a grain of relief at such news. After all, he and Sophia were lovers, not parents. But in his heart there was only deep regret and profound disappointment.

"So, I'll be leaving, then," Sophia said, her chin lifted. "As soon as the boat is finished, I'm heading to Baratin, then home."

Another shot of regret poked and prodded his heart at her statement, but with this, with her, he wouldn't acknowledge the feeling. It was best for her and for him that she go, follow the course she'd set for herself.

No matter how crazy it might make him.

He nodded in her direction, then turned to leave. ''I must return to my offices now.''

Under a gorgeous midafternoon sky, camped out on the grand lawns of the palace, under a shady cherry tree, Sophia took the white stick with its two blue lines out of her purse and stared down at it with a mixture of terror and wonderment.

She'd lied.

A child—Alex's child—was growing inside her, and she'd told him that her pregnancy test was negative.

Shame worked through her at a heady pace. She'd never done anything so horrid, so cruel, so selfish in her entire life. All in the name of fear.

After she'd heard him speak at the picnic last Saturday, heard the story of his unhappy past with a woman who had cared so little and taken so much, Sophia didn't want to add to his burden, give him something that he didn't want.

But all that had changed this morning when he'd told her that he wanted a child, just not the mother. Fear unlike anything she'd ever known had enveloped her. Alexander Thorne was a prince and a very powerful man. If he wanted to, he could take her child from her. All in the name of Llandaron.

This was so unlike her, she mused. She didn't run from problems.

Sophia plucked at the grass. Was she doing the right thing? For her child?

From behind her, something leaped at her shoulders. When she glanced back, a pink tongue darted out, lapped at her face.

The tension in her broke and she laughed out loud. "Well, how did you get here, little girl?"

The beautiful wolfhound pup cocked its head to the side and barked.

"Ahhh. Ran away, did you, Aggie?"

The answer came in the form of another lick to Sophia's face.

Smiling, Sophia stroked the pup's head. "Well, you're always welcome here."

On what could only be described as a contented sigh, Aggie did a double turn, then lay down, curled up at Sophia's side.

"Looks like she's got a crush on you, lass."

Sophia grinned. She knew that voice. Coming toward her on the lawn was Ranen and Alex's stunning aunt Fara. The older woman looked as if she just stepped off the pages of *Harper's Bazaar* with her chic short haircut and perfectly pressed white pantsuit.

"Ranen has been trying to get that pup to lie down all day," Fara informed her, a glowing smile about her lips.

Sophia threw up her hands. "I used no bargaining chip, I assure you. No bacon in these pockets."

Ranen snorted. "Likely story."

Fara pointed to the blanket spread out over the thick grass. "May we sit with you? This tree offers a lovely shade."

"Of course."

The twosome sat side by side, backs to the tree trunk, hands close but not touching.

Fara sighed as she looked about her. "You know, when Alex was a young boy, he would climb the cherry tree outside his window and sit up there for hours."

"You're kidding?"

"No. He was something of a dreamer."

"I can't imagine that."

Fara smiled and inclined her head. "Of course, he acted the somber child when we were near. His title and station demanded that it be so. But when he was alone, he could relax somewhat."

Ranen nodded his agreement with a taut jerk of the head. "He had his dreams, that one. He wanted a wife he could love, a brood of wee ones he could teach to explore and read and love the ocean as much as he does." The old man gave Sophia a look of cheerless understanding. "But he knew what was right—what had to be done."

"Which was marry a woman he didn't know?" Sophia asked, her voice sounding tired even to her own ears. "Have an heir? Rule his country?"

Ranen nodded. "Takes a disciplined mind."

"So all those dreams had to die?"

"Perhaps they didn't die." Fara smiled a little sadly. "Perhaps they were put aside. Until…"

"Until?" Sophia asked.

"Something or…someone came along to help him see those dreams once again."

A blush surged into Sophia's cheeks, and she looked down at the blanket, at the pup, anywhere but in the woman's eyes. She saw too much. What if she looked further and saw what was in Sophia's heart, all that she had done—and had not done?

*Until someone came along to help him see those dreams once again….*

Yes, she wanted Alex to find that part of himself again. That amazing, carefree part she'd so rarely seen. But was that her destiny? Was that *her* child's destiny?

To help a man who didn't want help?

Reaching out, Fara touched Sophia's hand. "You know, chances are best taken, my dear."

"I know," Sophia acquiesced. "It's just that—"

"You'd be wise to follow your own advice, Highness," Ranen interrupted.

The older woman looked over at him, startled, confused. "What in the world does that mean?"

Ranen suddenly jerked to his feet. "You know exactly what."

"I do not."

With a pained frown, the man turned and walked away, grumbling something Sophia couldn't make out.

"I'm sorry about that, my dear," Fara said, her voice weak.

Sophia felt the woman's hand tremble over her own. "Are you all right, Your Highness?"

"He is...he wants me to..." She shook her head. "I told you that chances were for taking. But I'm not altogether sure about second chances."

Fara said no more, and Sophia didn't push her. The two of them had heavy hearts and what were obviously difficult decisions to make. So as the sun began to vanish from the sky, casting the palatial grounds in shades of terra-cotta and gold, Sophia grasped Princess Fara's hand, hoping not only to give but to receive just a little bit of comfort.

It was half past eight that night when Alex walked through the door of the beach house. He felt weary and frustrated. His workday had been a slow, arduous one where all thoughts had raced to one subject and one subject only. Sophia. Like it or not, he couldn't get used to the idea of her leaving, and it made him insane that she had this power over him. This insatiable need he had to see her, hear her, touch her would not die no matter how hard he tried to—

"Hi, there. You hungry?"

The eagerness in her voice, the sweet welcome, made his chest constrict. "You must be a mind reader."

Her mouth curved into a smile. "That'll teach you to be careful of all those…thoughts you carry around with you."

"Are you picking up anything else?"

"Hmm." She cocked her head and glanced up at the ceiling as though trying to concentrate on his thoughts. It was all a coy little joke, but it sure gave Alex a moment to take her in.

Dressed in a navy-blue knit dress, feet bare, her hair pulled back in a loose ponytail and soft makeup on her flawless face, she looked incredibly beautiful—elegant yet casual—every round curve she possessed shown off to perfection.

"Oh, my," she exclaimed suddenly. "I've just picked up on something."

"Wild thoughts?"

"And wicked."

"Well, that's the trouble with being around you."

She looked puzzled.

A chuckle escaped Alex's throat. "Wild and wicked thoughts are a guaranteed occurrence."

"Oh." Stains of pink appeared on her cheeks. "Well, thank you, I think."

"Make no mistake, Sophia," he said, walking toward her until he was just a foot away. "That was a compliment."

"And I'm betting that you say stuff like that to all the girls." She grinned, shrugged. "Or princesses or countesses or whatever you date."

"I don't date. And no, I rarely tell a woman my thoughts—sexual or otherwise."

She appeared shocked by his bold honesty, as he was himself. He didn't tell a woman his thoughts. So why had he told this woman? She was no princess, no countess, just a green-eyed, red-haired commoner from San Diego, California who had stolen his control the moment he'd laid eyes on her.

"Why don't we sit?" Sophia suggested, taking a step back, showing him the dining table fully dressed up with plates and wineglasses and a pot with steam wafting out. "The stew's getting cold."

"Stew. Good God, I haven't had stew in thirty years."

"You don't like it?" she asked, melancholy lacing her tone.

"No. Love it." He took off his jacket and sat down at the table. "I just haven't had the pleasure of late. Hearty, earthy dishes are rarely served at social functions or at the pretentious restaurants I'm forced to frequent."

"Of course."

"A grave error, I've always thought."

She gave him a soft, appreciative smile, then sat down beside him, not across from him as he would've expected, but beside him. And the gesture pleased him immensely.

"I know good politics when I hear it," she teased, ladling him out a healthy helping of stew. "You're a wonderful diplomat, Alex, and you're just trying to make me feel good about serving peasant food to a prince."

Alex couldn't help himself. He eased a finger under her chin and lifted her gaze to his. "If I was trying to make you feel good—" he leaned in, kissed her softly on the lips "—there are so many better ways."

"Are there?" she asked breathlessly, her gaze shifting to his mouth. "Like what, for instance?"

He grinned and leaned toward her. But this time instead of kissing her he took her lower lip between his teeth and gently tugged. A soft moan escaped her throat, and her eyes remained closed.

The ache inside him raged like an animal. He wanted more, and clearly so did she, but he wasn't about to ravage her at the dinner table—not when she'd gone to all the trouble of making him dinner.

No, he would wait until later.

"You taste like heaven, Sophia," he said, sitting back. He snatched up his spoon and dug into the stew. "And this is heavenly," he murmured again before slipping a spoonful of stew into his mouth. "Thank you."

Sophia watched him eat, her own appetite defunct. But from the kiss or the lie she'd told that morning, she wasn't sure. What she did know for certain was that it was time to stop running.

Today, sitting beside Fara, she'd really thought about what she'd done and said—and had not said—to Alex. She'd realized that her reasons for deceiving him, no matter how just they'd felt at the time, were cowardly. And she was no coward. Her child deserved a family. And Alex deserved the chance to be a father.

He didn't love her, she knew, but surely he wouldn't keep her from their child. At least, she prayed he wouldn't.

Sophia waited until Alex was finished with his meal, with his wine, then took a breath and jumped. "I have something I have to tell you, Alex."

He drained his wine glass. "This sounds serious."

"It is."

"Your boat is going to take another month for repairs?"

She was set to flinch, ready to reply with something quick and cool, thinking his words were meant unkindly. But when her eyes met his, so hot, needful, soulful, she realized he hadn't meant his query as a concern. In fact, the expression on his face was one of hope. He wanted her just as she wanted him. Neither one of them was ready for this...this whatever-it-was between them to come to an end.

There was nothing she wanted to do more than take his hand and lead him into her bedroom, beg him to make love to her all night. Her body craved him, and she was through denying it. But before she could be intimate with him again, she had to tell him the truth.

"What is it, Sophia? What's wrong?"

Shame filled her soul, but there was nothing for it. "This morning when I told you the pregnancy test was negative..."

As her voice faded, so did the heat from Alex's eyes. Apprehension took up quick residence.

"Continue," he said, his tone now commanding, all arrogance, as though he were speaking to a servant who was about to make a confession.

With every ounce of strength she had in her, she forced out the words. "I lied to you."

"What?" he fairly hissed.

"It wasn't true...what I said. It—"

"You...you are..."

"Yes. I'm pregnant, Alex."

He pushed away from the table with such force, his water glass capsized and dropped to the floor with a crash. Sophia stared at the broken glass, at the water as it seeped into all the cracks and crevices of the floor. She felt as though she'd just broken something in Alex, and in them, with her admission.

"How could you do this?" he demanded, glaring at her burning, reproachful eyes.

She felt as if her breath was cut off, but she stumbled on. "My only excuse—if that even matters now—is that I was scared."

"Of what?"

"The future. My future, the child's future."

"Your future?"

"Yes. I want to be with my child—"

His eyes narrowed dangerously. "If there really is a child. You've lied to me once, Sophia, how do I know you're telling me the truth now?"

Silently Sophia reached into her purse, took out the test and boldly held it out to him.

He snatched it up on a growl, then scanned the white stick with its two blue lines as though looking for the fine print. When he saw what he needed to see, he released a weighty breath. "This changes everything, you have to know that."

"I know that this child is your child. And I understand what that means."

Concern had surpassed the anger in his gaze. "Do you, Sophia?"

"Maybe not to the full extent. But I realize that we'll have to live here in Llandaron—"

"Not just in Llandaron."

"What do you mean?"

"The child must live with me."

"Alex, let's not get ahead of—"

"As will you."

"Alex—"

"Sophia," he said, every angle and line and plane of his body proclaiming his demand, "you must marry me."

# Seven

The mattress felt like bricks tonight, unyielding and unforgiving.

Sophia threw back the covers, allowed the cool night air rushing through her windows to brush over her skin. Normally, the sound and smell and caress of the ocean breeze did wonders for her bruised psyche.

But not tonight.

She glanced at her bedside clock. Midnight.

Just four hours ago she'd confessed her secret to Alex. And after the initial anger and shock had worn down, she'd listened as he'd told her that they were to be married.

Heck, with that kind of shock, of course the breeze wasn't doing much but keeping her cool.

So used to having his commands met, Alex hadn't even given the idea over to discussion or refusal. He'd simply walked out the front door, headed down to the beach and stayed there for hours. Sophia had heard him come in after she was in bed.

Married to the crown prince of Llandaron, she mused. Married to Alex. An uneasy smile graced her lips. Yes, she wanted this man. Yes, she wanted to raise her child with its father. But the uncertain future ahead filled her with fear. As did the uncertain feelings of a certain prince. What did he want? What did he really want?

Clearly, he was acting on instinct and protocol. Maybe marrying the mother of the heir to the throne of Llandaron was a law or something. Who knew. But Sophia didn't come from that kind of world; arranged marriages to royals, men and ladies of the court you'd spoken to once or twice, stuff like that. In her world you married the person you were in love with or not at all.

Sitting up, Sophia swung her legs over the side of the bed. Maybe Alex wasn't willing to talk to her about this future he'd already dictated, but she sure as hell couldn't allow the sun to come up on another day without some kind of understanding.

Clad in a thin white tank and blue pajama bottoms,

she made her way down the hall to his room. But once outside the door, she paused for a moment.

If she wasn't sleeping, odds were he wasn't, either, right?

She knocked softly on his door.

She heard him sigh, then utter a husky, "This isn't a wise idea, Sophia."

"We need to talk, Alex."

"Go back to sleep."

"I'm not sleeping. I can't sleep. Obviously you can't, either." And with that, she opened the door and walked inside, no permission, no thought.

A grave mistake.

A fire blazed in the black marble hearth beside the mahogany four-poster, illuminating the man in the bed to knee-buckling perfection.

Chest ripped with sinewy muscle, arms powerful and lightly tanned, Alex lay there, his back to the ornately carved headboard, watching her, totally nude, save for a navy-blue silk sheet lightly draped over his hips. His black hair was mussed, his jaw darkened with stubble, and his eyes shone like two brilliant and very sensual amethysts.

Without reserve, Sophia stared longingly at him, wishing she could join him, wanting him to open his arms and command her to bed.

"I told you this was unwise," Alex said, his lips twisted into a cynical smile.

"Why? Because you're in bed with no clothes on?"

"Something like that, yes."

"I'm not embarrassed, Alex." Desperately turned on, she thought inanely, but not embarrassed.

"Good to know."

"After all, we've seen…each other…"

He snorted, laced his hands behind his head. "Following that line of logic, I think it's only fair that you remove your clothes, as well."

"Excuse me?" she fairly choked.

"It's only fair, don't you think?"

"Aren't you too angry with me to want me?"

His gaze raked boldly over her. "I don't think that's possible. I don't think I could ever be that angry."

Sophia's heart jolted—or maybe the sensation came from someplace below her abdomen, deep within her core.

This setting, fire and ocean waves, broad shoulders and eyes that tugged at her clothes as much as they tugged at her heart…it was so disturbing. If it was possible, her skin actually ached for him, ached for his touch. Every inch of her calling out to every inch of him. When? Now? *Yes…*

But she couldn't take even if he was willing to give. Not yet. Not until they worked out this crazy marriage command he'd tossed her way.

"Alex we need to talk."

He gestured to the edge of the bed. "Have a seat."

"I'm fine standing."

"Don't be ridiculous. You look chilled. The fire is warmer over here."

Warm? Right, she mused. Try blazing, scorching, inferno. Try...

Irresistible.

But like a kid to candy, she went, walked over to the side of his mahogany "throne," sat down on blue silk and tried not to breathe differently.

"Now," Alex began, still sprawled back against the headboard, hands behind his head, chest wide and splendid, attitude commanding. "What has you coming to my room at midnight?"

"This subject of marriage."

"What about it?"

"Let's get serious."

"I assure you, Sophia, I was nothing if not serious."

She asked the silly question she'd posed in her mind earlier. "Is there some kind of law stating that you have to marry your child's mother?"

"There is no law."

"Then we don't have to be married to share a child, do we?"

"Granted, there is no legal basis for my decision, but we *are* talking about the monarchy here. There are unspoken rules we live with, and we must abide by them." He released his hands from behind his head and crossed his arms over his chest. "This is not a contemporary situation, Sophia. My child will be heir to the throne. He or she must be brought into a union, not a single-parent home."

"You are really ready to go through with this again? Marry a woman you don't love for your country?" She waited with bated breath for his answer. And it came quick, and painful.

"Not for my country, for my child," he corrected, pride in his tone.

"A worthy sacrifice for your child. Marrying its mother." She hated the bitter tone in her voice, hated it and was embarrassed by it. But, Lord, she understood this man's reasoning, too. She would give up anything for her sweet baby as well.

"Sophia?"

"Yes?"

"Don't make the mistake of thinking that I have no feeling for you."

She put a hand up in protest. "Alex, you don't need to—"

"It is true that I cannot love you," he interrupted. "I don't have that capability, that gift. 'Tis a lost gene." He shrugged. "But there is something between us. Call it what you will—heat, need, desire—"

"All physical."

He shook his head. "Not necessarily. Need and desire can reach far past the physical."

So, he cared about her, liked her, needed her in some cosmic way. But the truth remained that he wouldn't be offering her marriage if she wasn't pregnant.

Her mind showcased a telling slide show, with pictures from the afternoon the *Daydream* hit a rock all the way up to now, sitting on Alex's bed.

She put her head in her hands and sighed. "I can't believe I've allowed all this to happen."

"That may be the case, Sophia, but it is happening. And we must do what's best for the child now, yes?"

"Of course. Yes. I just—"

"Good. Then it's settled. Our child will come into a family."

Sophia glanced up, into the fire, her heart squeezing painfully. A family. For almost a year she'd been without the only family she'd ever really loved. She was lonely. And God help her she wanted the whole Thorne Clan. But what was more important, her baby deserved them.

"Sophia, what are you thinking?"

She turned to look at him, all handsome and royal and…unattainable. "That I would sacrifice anything for my child. Even my own…"

"What? Happiness? Desires?"

"Yes."

"I can satisfy one right now if you'll allow me."

Her heart skipped, literally, skipped a beat. This man's appeal was devastating, and to fall into his arms sounded like pure heaven right now. But was it enough? Would she regret it later when she was lying beside him thinking about what he could never give her?

But the answer didn't surface within her, and she felt too tired to search for it.

She stood up. "I think we're done here."

He bowed his head. "Waiting until the wedding night. Yes, much better."

"Good-night, Alex," she said firmly.

He grinned. "Pleasant dreams, Sophia."

And as her pulse skittered in her heated blood, Sophia walked away from her future husband, out of his bedroom, making sure to close the door securely behind her.


"I like the cream chiffon."

"The pale-green silk is so beautiful on her," Cathy said, holding up the dress in question.

Fran gaped at her. "Green silk? She can't wear green on her wedding day."

"Why not?"

"Ladies," Sophia said from her perch at the edge of Cathy's hand-carved sleigh bed. "Let's try and remember that this whole thing is a charade not a romantic moment in time."

Both women stopped what they were doing, turned away from the full-length mirror and promptly gave Sophia two very child-like frowns.

Sophia couldn't help but laugh, though the sound was anything but gay. "I'm just saying, let's be realistic here."

"I'm being realistic." Fran cocked an eyebrow. "You *are* falling for him, Sophia, and to me that's pretty darn romantic."

Cathy nodded, hugging the green silk dress closer to her chest. "And he's definitely falling in love with—"

"Don't say it," Sophia interrupted dauntingly. "Don't even think it. He's marrying me for our child."

It had been Sophia's intention to keep her pregnancy a secret, at least for a while, at least until Alex could tell his father. But around Fran and Cathy, she felt as though secrets were an impossibility. The terrific twosome brought out a bonding, sisterly impulse in her. And wrong or right, she'd just wanted to tell them that she was one of them now. So, when they'd picked her up to go shopping that morning, she'd spilled the entire thing.

All about the baby and the marriage.

Cathy and Fran couldn't have been more delighted or more supportive. Just as they were being now, Sophia thought with a melancholy smile.

Fran pitched the cream chiffon over a chair and came to sit beside Sophia on the bed. "Perhaps the baby is the impetus for the marriage, but—"

Sophia shook her head. "He told me quite clearly that he's incapable of love."

"That's just fear talking," Cathy assured her, placing the green dress over the cream and joining them on the edge of her bed. "You must understand this, if Alex lets his guard down, if he acknowledges his true feelings for you, he could be hurt again."

"What do you mean?" Sophia asked.

Cathy touched her shoulder. "He didn't love his ex-wife, but he certainly cared for her and tried to make the relationship work."

"And look what happened," Fran finished. "She walked out on him, humiliated him, made him feel as though he'd lost control and couldn't trust himself or anyone else again. Wouldn't you be scared to listen to your heart, put yourself on the line again, too?"

"Of course, but—"

"Give him a chance," Cathy urged, coming to her feet. "Give this marriage a chance. It could be the best decision of your life."

A wave of hope washed over Sophia as she listened to Cathy and Fran. Alex *had* been through hell, and he was gun-shy now. That was understandable. But the question still remained; past or future, could he ever relinquish that control that bound him and fall in love with her?

No one was capable of answering that question today. Right now, she just needed to focus on the present. On creating the best family she could. And if she was lucky enough to find, to have, what Cathy and Fran had, she would be forever thankful.

With a flash of smile at her new sisters—her new family—Sophia said merrily, ''I think we should go with the green silk.''

Here he was. Once again. Dressed in princely robes and stern expression, standing in front of the same priest who had performed his marriage rites the last time—that fateful time.

Alex inhaled deeply, calling for calm.

This time was different though. He had to admit it. Instead of the one thousand friends and relatives that had been in attendance five years ago, today there were only a mere 150 gathered in the ancient palace church.

Aside from the drop in number of invited guests, this time Alex had no misconceptions about his marriage, no hopes for an impossible future and a beautiful child already on the way.

He also had her.

The vision that stood before him.

As the priest continued with his wedding sermon, Alex took in the view. Beneath a veil of pale-green tulle and crystals, Sophia smiled tentatively up at him.

Never in his life had he seen a woman so lovely. She wore a floor-length dress of pale-green silk that clung to every curve she possessed, yet upheld the modesty the day dictated. Her long red hair hung loose about her shoulders in soft curls, and her skin glowed with health and the beginning of pregnancy. But what really made his body ache for her, were her lips, full and rosy and just a little bit moist.

A bitter chuckle rose in his throat. He'd wanted to feel absolutely nothing today. But that idea had been thoroughly crushed when he'd seen his bride walking down the aisle toward him. Like the fool that he was, he'd felt too much. He'd felt attracted, mindful and incredibly protective of her.

"Do you take this woman..." The priest interrupted Alex's thoughts as his crackly query boomed through the hushed church.

Did he take this woman?

Had the man of God heard him, seen the pictures in his mind, Alex wondered inanely? Yes, he wanted to take this woman. Bloody hell, he wanted—

The priest inclined his head, whispered, "Your Highness?"

Alex brushed aside all thought for a moment and answered the old man. "Yes, I do."

"And Sophia Rebecca Dunhill," the priest continued. "Do you take this man as your husband? To love him, honor him and obey him..."

Sophia arched a brow at him when the priest said, "obey him."

Alex grinned at her, couldn't help himself. He wondered if she would say yes to everything but the promise to obey. She was so spirited, so passionate, and she would give him trouble always. But damn if he didn't like that about her.

Sophia was looking straight at him, her eyes clearly saying she didn't plan to obey anyone at anytime, but her smile was warm. "Yes. I do."

"Then by the power vested in me by God, I pronounce you husband and wife. You may kiss your bride, Your Highness."

Alex's chest felt as if it would burst. His bride, his wife. A shadow rushed through him, sallow and anxious. But he fought it. He fought it because a welcome pleasure was now upon him.

Reverently Alex lifted his bride's veil. "Your Highness," he whispered before lowering his head and covering her mouth, giving her a tender kiss.

She tasted like sweet mint, and he wanted so much more. But he only took a moment, as they were in church with the eyes of all his acquaintances and relatives upon them. Then he grasped her hand in his and guided her down the aisle and out into the vast courtyard where the afternoon reception was to take place.

White roses and purple heather sprung up everywhere. In vases on the tables, in oak barrels bordering the antediluvian courtyard. Servants wandered in and out serving champagne and caviar on toast. Guests milled about drinking and eating and, Alex mused, no doubt comparing this wedding to the last.

When the king, dressed in all his impressive royal

plumage, made his entrance, the assembly bowed low. He hastily waved them back to their celebration and headed across the courtyard. His eyes bright, he made his way over to Alex and his bride.

Alex shook his head in bewilderment at the beaming smile of his father's face. Oddly enough, the man hadn't reacted at all foully to the news of his marriage or the child he'd conceived with Sophia. In fact, he'd actually asked if he could have his staff take care of all the wedding details.

"Sophia," the king fairly gushed, taking both her hands in his. "You are one of my daughters now. I hope this pleases you as much as it pleases me."

"It does, Your Majesty," Sophia returned earnestly. Smiling a little sadly, she added, "I lost my own father when I was a child, then last year…"

"Ah, yes, Ranen's brother."

She nodded.

"Not to worry, my dear. Now you have us both. Two old grumps looking out for your welfare."

"Thank you. I'm truly honored, sire."

"Well, if that's the case, we must have a dance." The king looked at Alex. "If your husband has no objection."

The word gripped Alex's heart like a vise. "No objection at all."

Alex watched as his father took Sophia out to the floor for a slow waltz, watched as Ranen guided Fara to the floor to join them, watched as the guests followed suit. Soon, everyone was dancing.

Almost everyone, at any rate.

"Congratulations, brother." Maxim came up to stand beside him, beer in hand. "But shouldn't that be you out there dancing?"

"I'm no dancer, as you know."

"True enough." Maxim sighed as he stared at the dance floor. "Sophia's quite a beauty."

Alex nodded. "She is that."

Sidling up to Alex on the opposite side, Dan cuffed his brother-in-law on the shoulder. "Wife and child. You're really one of us now."

"It would seem so."

"Ah, the joys of pregnancy," Maxim regaled. "Morning sickness—"

"Mood swings," Dan offered on a chuckle.

"Late-night fudge cravings."

Dan shook his head. "We haven't had those. It's been fried chicken for Cathy."

"Sounds rather taxing," Alex said, his voice calm, his gaze steady as he watched a Spanish duke ask Sophia to dance.

Dan snorted. "Don't let our typical male complaints deceive you, buddy. We love every minute of it, don't we, Max?"

"It's true. Nothing's better than having the woman you love carrying your child."

His brother's words stung, straight to his very soul. "Yes…" Alex uttered coolly.

"What's with the long face, Alex?" Dan chided good-naturedly. "You hit the jackpot today."

If that Spanish bastard held Sophia any closer, Alex thought darkly, he would rather enjoy breaking both the man's legs. True, he'd never taken to dancing. So what. That Spaniard had no right to take such liberties with his wife. Maybe Prince Alexander Thorne wasn't capable of love, but he sure as hell was capable of jealousy.

Sophia was his now, for better, for worse, forever.

But when she glanced over at Alex, her eyes imploring him to come to her, dance with her himself, he turned away. Jealousy was a weakness he couldn't afford. Not now, not ever, if he was going to stay sane and strong in this marriage. He couldn't afford to have her see such an emotion as jealousy in him. He'd already given up too much control and was already too bloody involved with her as it was.

Alex turned to his brother, did something that he would never have dreamed of doing. "I need some air."

"What?" Maxim exclaimed.

"I'm going back to the beach house."

"Alex what the hell? You can't just leave your bride here by her—"

Alex's lip curled. "Please don't tell me what I can and cannot do, little brother."

True, leaving this reception was uncalled for and completely devoid of his customary sense of duty. But he didn't care. The first marriage and the second were fusing in his mind, making him mad. He needed to detach himself.

"Alex," Dan began, his voice smooth and relaxed as though he were trying to pass those traits off onto a foolish groom. "Why don't we all have a drink and relax."

"Thanks, but I'll be drinking alone tonight."

He turned to leave, but Maxim grabbed his arm. "You don't care how this will look?"

"I will tell the king that urgent business has called me away."

"But what should we tell Sophia?"

Alex shrugged him off and muttered a terse, "Anything you want," before walking away.

# Eight

A brilliant sphere of moon lit the beach with a ghostly glow. Though she felt almost desperate to get to him, Sophia took patient steps toward the living statue that faced the tortured ocean waves.

Arms crossed over his chest, legs splayed, jaw tight, Alex didn't even glance at her when she came to stand beside him.

"I thought I'd find you here," Sophia said casually.

"Why did you come looking?"

She didn't flinch at his curt reply. After all, it wasn't in her nature to cower when others got angry or impassioned. Besides, this man was her husband now, with all his flaws and all his fears.

"Alex, you know why I'm here." Her mind whirred with reasons, with truths. She wanted to tell him that she cared about him and knew that he was uneasy over the leap they'd just taken. But she could tell he wasn't ready to hear that.

So she grinned and said, "I needed to get out of there. Your father can throw one crazy party. The band actually refused to play any more waltzes until the bandleader performed a rap song."

"Is that so?" he said dryly.

"No." She rolled her eyes, sighed. Obviously, humor wasn't going to work, either. "That's not so. The truth is, I was ticked off that you left me back there with your entire family and a hundred of your closest friends, and I wanted to give you a good dressing down."

After a moment he turned to look at her, his eyes a strange mixture of frustration and heat. "You want to give me a dressing down, huh?"

A delightful shiver of sensuality moved through her. "Something like that."

"Well, perhaps we should go inside then."

She shook her head, though her feminine instinct hovered briefly over his suggestion. "No, not yet. We need to settle this. I want to know why you walked out on our reception."

"I had something I needed to take care of."

"Right, you had a business emergency." She snorted. "Oh, please."

Alex's eyebrows shot up in surprise. "Is that what Maxim told you?"

"He could barely look me in the eye when he said it."

"Hmm. Perhaps I shouldn't have put such a burden on him."

"Perhaps not." She cracked a smile, wanting to be irritated with him but finding it impossible. "You know, you're entirely too cocky, Your Highness."

Something close to a grin tugged at his mouth. "Yes, I know."

As the waves hit the shore, Sophia sighed. She wasn't sure which direction to take here, how best to get through to him. But she had to try something. "Alex, if this is going to work, don't you think we should at least try and be friends?"

"I don't want you as a friend."

"You're not being reasonab—"

"I said I don't want you as a friend."

"How do you want me, then?" she exclaimed, gathering frustration now.

"Dammit, Sophia!"

"What?"

He groaned, his eyes flashing in a familiar display of impatience. "This line of conversation is making me insane. Why are you here? What is it that you want from me?"

"I just want you to talk to me."

"About what?"

With a quick shrug, she said, "I'm a good listener, and maybe talking about your past, about your feelings, could really help."

Through gritted teeth, he uttered, "I'm not looking to be saved from the past."

"What, then? Are you looking to hold on to all that stuff with your ex-wife as protection or something?"

His laugh was forced, bleak. "I thought you were a writer not a psychiatrist."

Never in her life had Sophia been in such a battle of wills with such a formidable partner. Her grandfather was a stubborn man, but not like this. Not completely closed off to feeling and pain and history.

Obviously, Crown Prince Alexander wasn't used to giving in to anyone. But she was growing tired of fighting him.

"All right, Alex," she said, turning away, ready to head back up to the house. "You win. I won't beg."

But she didn't get very far. Alex's hand darted out and caught her wrist, turned her to face him. "Bloody hell, Sophia. Don't you understand? I'm the one who wants to beg here."

"You?"

"You sound shocked."

"I am. I can't imagine you ever resorting to something so—"

"So what?" He suddenly pulled her close to him, body to body, as the ocean breeze swirled the skirt of her wedding dress around them. "So base? Desperate? Humble?"

"No. So honest."

He stiffened as though she'd struck him. Cursed as if he'd been wounded. Then after a moment, he lowered his head, pausing just centimeters before taking her mouth. "I am being honest. I've never denied wanting you. Not to you or to myself."

Sophia could hardly get her breath. Her entire body was reacting to the closeness of him, his clean, spicy masculine scent, his heart-wrenching frustration. "This has escalated past the physical, don't you agree?"

A thin, tight muscle pulsated under the skin below his jaw as he whispered huskily, "It cannot."

"Do you think this is easy for me, either, Alex?"

He didn't answer, merely nuzzled her lips with his own, causing her lips to part and a rush of wet heat to pool low at her core.

She struggled to speak, tasting him as she went, feeling as though her mind had fled time and reason and was now drifting with the waves behind them. "I've lost everyone I've ever loved in my life. Do you think I want to become attached to someone? Trust someone? Open myself up to getting hurt again?"

"I would never hurt—"

"Don't make that promise."

His hands raked up her back and into her hair. "Sophia, you lost your family through natural causes, not because they didn't want to stay—''

"But my pride is still at stake," she said roughly. "This marriage is terrifying and risky for both of us. But we've done it, Alex. I've spoken my vows, and I know this—I won't run from you…ever.''

His hands fisted in her hair. "And you don't make that promise.''

"I can," she insisted, pressing her hips against him, feeling the rock-hard evidence of his need. "I can because I want you that much.''

"Sophia…''

"At least I have the guts to go after what I want.''

"Damn you!''

He said no more, just scooped her up in his arms as though she weighed little more than a grain of sand and stalked back to the beach house.

The last time they'd been together, their lovemaking had been quick, wild, even a little dangerous.

But this time, Sophia promised herself, as Alex carried her into the bedroom, this time they would go slow. Enjoying each other without reproach or thought or worry because they both desperately needed this reconnection.

The distance to the bed was little, but Alex didn't ease her down on the mattress as she expected. No, he was a man of surprises and sensation, and when he let her down, it was to stand in front of him. It was to look at her, take her in, drink her in with those woman-killer eyes of his.

"You looked so beautiful today," he said, his tone rough and ragged. "When you came down that aisle, I nearly lost my mind."

She offered him a coy smile. "I'm sorry for that."

"No, you're not." The full moon outside the bay window gave off their only light, but it was enough to see Alex's wicked grin.

Sophia shook her head. "No, you're right, I'm not sorry."

In one stride, he moved to stand behind her. Missing him, his warmth, she started to turn toward him, but he stopped her with one word.

"Please."

Such a statement coming from that mouth made her freeze, made the excitement in her build all the more. What was next? What was he going to do next?

"This is our wedding night, Sophia," he whispered close to her ear as he started unbuttoning her dress, his fingers cool against each inch of skin he exposed. "This is our wedding night and I have no gift."

"You don't need to give me anything," she assured him, her breathing heavy with longing.

"Yes, I do. You deserve all for marrying a man like me."

Sophia's heart ached for his pain and torment, just as her skin ached for his touch. He had everything a man could ask for: riches, power, the adoration of thousands. But his sense of worth and his pride had been twisted by a horrible marriage.

He wanted more from this marriage, more from Sophia than he would ever admit—she knew that as well as she knew her own name. But she also knew she would have to be patient, loving, tender and open to get him to see the truth. Maybe then he would take what she was so willing to give.

At that thought, her silk dress fell into a sea-green pool on the floor. Cool air rushed her skin and she pressed her back against his chest, looking for his arms to fold around her. But Alex wasn't finished removing her clothing. With deft fingers, he flicked the clasp of her bra, lifted the lacy straps from her shoulders and let that, too, drop to the hardwood floor.

Sophia sucked in a breath as she felt his hands move lower, his fingers finding the edge of the white lacy thong Fran had insisted she wear. With a gentle tug, he eased her panties down, over her hips, down her thighs and ankles until she was totally naked before him.

"No gift," he uttered again as he reached around her waist, palming her abdomen.

Sophia placed her hand over his, at the place where his child grew inside her. "This is the best gift you could ever give me."

"Sophia, lass," he uttered hoarsely, his kisses searing her neck and shoulders while he moved his hand lower, then lower still.

A moan, guttural and fierce ripped from Sophia's throat as Alex's fingers slipped between the silken curls at the junction of her thighs.

"Open your legs for me," he whispered in her ear.

He needed the control like he needed to breathe.

And she gave it to him.

She pressed herself back into him again, this time feeling his erection, hard and pulsating against the top of her buttocks. On a purely feminine growl of satisfaction, she did as he commanded, stepping out, parting her legs for him.

A trembling sensation came over her as he reached around, cupped her breast, kneading the plump flesh, while his other hand palmed her, then penetrated her, slipping first one finger, then a second inside her. Liquid honey met him, and she heard his sharp intake of breath next to her ear.

"Hold yourself open for me, Sophia," he commanded.

A soft whisper of embarrassment gripped her heart. She'd never been touched this way, never been so exposed. But she was falling head over heels in love with this man. He was her husband, her lover, and if she ever wanted him to be free with her, she would have to set the tone, here and now.

Her breath shallow, she eased her hands down her stomach, way down to the center of her body and did as he asked, parting her slick, pink folds for him.

"So hard," he whispered in her ear as he rolled

one aching nipple between his fingers. "So wet," he said as he used his thumb to stroke the very core of her.

Sophia was starting to feel as though she couldn't stand on her own anymore, couldn't give to anyone but herself anymore. Electricity and heat surged through her abdomen, the pulsating sensation almost painful.

But she took the wondrous pain, bucking against his fingers, moaning into the sea air rushing through the window, knowing that she couldn't hold on, hold back much longer. She could only surrender to him as she was surrendering to her love for him.

Suddenly, shudders of pleasure hit her full on, sending a wave of heat screaming through her body.

Her breathing became ragged as she took it all, reveled in it all. And when the convulsions eased, she felt depleted—yet wanted more.

She wanted Alex.

Whirling on him, she gripped the back of his neck and pulled his mouth down to hers. Her kiss was hungry and demanding as her fingers inched up, threading into his hair. She felt his erection straining against his pants, pressing into her belly. There was something so erotic about being naked when he was fully dressed, but the need to feel him, all of him was too strong to deny.

She fumbled with his jacket, the buttons on his

pants, but she was too slow, too awkward. And she wanted his mouth again.

Alex must've heard her silent plea, because he gathered her in his arms, slanting his mouth over hers, taking her tongue into his mouth, playing and giving and tormenting as he moved them onto the bed.

Her back licking the cool silk sheets, she watched as he ripped off his jacket, watched as his eyes turned a smoky shade of wine, smiled as he gazed down at her hungrily.

Slowly he eased over her, gave her a slow, drugging kiss on the mouth before dipping his head to her breasts.

How could he be this loving with her, she wondered, this open about his wants and needs, yet keep his heart so closed?

The query left as quickly as it came, for Alex was drawing slow, lazy circles around her breast with his tongue. Sophia let her head fall back, her eyes close as he made his way slowly, so slowly, to the hardened peak. And when he did, when he laved her nipple, then suckled it deep into his mouth, she cried out.

Perfect torture.

She arched her back, her hips, anything to tell him that she wanted him closer, inside her body where he'd be warm and safe.

He glanced up then, as if he'd heard her thoughts, his gaze fierce. "Tell me you want me, Sophia."

"So much, Alex," she said, her tone impassioned.

"Tell me this is okay for our child. We aren't hurting—"

"No, it's perfectly fine."

He stood then, stripped himself of pants and boxers, then eased her legs apart. As he moved over her, his hands slowly raked up her inner thighs, massaging as he went. Sophia hummed with need, anticipation, her memory roaring back to the first time he'd been inside her. The heat, the sensation, the—

Alex entered her with one silky stroke, filling her with thick, hard steel and a tenderness he would never admit to. But she could feel him, his desire and his heart beating inside her.

She wrapped her legs around his waist, moving with him as he started off with slow, heady strokes that soon graduated to raw, ravenous thrusts.

The core of her, that small bundle of nerves Alex had taken to heaven earlier was shimmering with heat once again. Her nails digging into his back, she slammed her hips upward over and over, reveling in the sound of their bodies slapping with slick play.

A guttural sound escaped Alex's throat and he covered her mouth with his as he went deep, surged deep, then shattered with the intensity of his climax.

A second later Sophia followed him.

Sunlight lumbered through the window, bathing the room in lazy beams of white. Tagging along, came a soft ocean breeze, urging the navy curtains bracketing the window into a graceful dance.

Eyes still closed, Alex reached up and stretched. He hadn't felt this good, this relaxed in a long time. If ever. Last night Sophia had been wild and wanting and completely giving of herself without embarrassment or shame. Highly addictive.

His bride, his wife.

Alex waited for the unease of her new title to wash over him. But it didn't. Instead, it settled deep in his bones, seemingly content with just being fact. Strange. And a little bit disconcerting.

Surely one night of glorious lovemaking hadn't turned his mind from his vow. No, he still coveted control. He could have both, he quickly assured himself. The warmth of his wife without the push for self-discovery, forgiveness and promises.

Just the very thought of warmth and his wife had Alex's blood pumping hard. He knew he had given her a new experience last night, and he wanted to give her more, anything she desired. Anytime she desired it.

But when he opened his eyes, reached for her to give her that pleasure, he found only sheets and the space beside him empty as a tomb.

A straining sense of doom clawed at his gut. One he couldn't shake off even as he jolted out bed and headed for the living room.

Once there, doom turned to agitation. She was nowhere in sight. Nor was she in the bathroom, kitchen or out on the beach.

The clock above the stove struck eight. Where had she gone so early on a Saturday? On the morning of their first day as husband and wife.

Answers came, ones he didn't want, ones that were so embedded in his mind now, that they couldn't be shut off. Had she lied last night about staying with him? he wondered, anger and misery saturating his senses. Had she had second thoughts about their marriage, about raising their child amongst royalty—with him?

His lips thinned dangerously. Had she walked out just as—

"Morning, Highness."

Alex turned sharply at the singsong call, caught his smiling and incredibly beautiful wife in the doorway.

"Where have you been?" he asked, his tone excessively harsh even to his own ears.

"Someone woke up on the wrong side of the royal bed this morning." From behind her back, she pulled out a basket. "I was just out hunting for some breakfast. We have nothing in the fridge."

He heard her words, but they did little to appease him. He started to pace. "You shouldn't go out alone. You're the crown princess of Llandaron now."

"Relax. I went into town, grabbed a few things and headed back. No harm done."

"No harm done?" he said through gritted teeth.

"You could've been kidnapped or worse. You must understand your—"

"My what? My place?"

"Yes!"

"Alex, I'm going to pretend I didn't hear you say that." She walked over to the counter, set the basket down and started unpacking. "I'm guessing this isn't really about me being kidnapped. But I suppose you aren't going to tell me what it *is* about, right?"

She was too bloody patient, too grounded, and she saw far too much. He continued to pace, barking, "There is nothing more to tell."

"Right. Okay. Let me just say then that this princess thing is new and unfamiliar territory, and from now on I'll have a palace guard with me if I go into town alone." She glanced over her shoulder at him. "All right?"

He mumbled a terse "Fine" her way, then asked briskly, "So, what did you trek into town for?"

She rolled her eyes and smiled. "Blueberry biscuits and honey butter."

Alex stopped dead in his tracks, his heart twisting inside his chest. "How in the world could you…"

"Your favorite breakfast, right?"

She'd done it. That one, very sweet, very intimate act she'd just performed was the stopper in his bottle of restraint, the bottle he'd reluctantly left open to breathe the moment he'd met her.

Finding out about his favorite breakfast, that was something a wife did for her…husband.

But they were husband and wife, he quickly reminded himself.

It was just that, such a gesture—it was what a *loving* wife did for her husband.

Alex stalked over to her, looked into her eyes. Did she love him? He knew she cared for him, was attracted to him, but love…

''Why would you do this?'' he asked, searching her gaze.

She frowned. ''What do you mean 'why'? Because I thought you'd enjoy it.''

He couldn't allow her to love him.

''I appreciate the gesture, Sophia.'' His tone was tight and forced. ''But you—''

She dropped onto one of the bar stools with a huff, her patience obviously draining. ''But I crossed the invisible and ever-changing line you've drawn between yourself and the rest of the world, is that it?''

''I just don't want there to be any confusion.''

''Confusion over what?''

''No matter what we do in there,'' he said, pointing toward the bedroom. ''You must never forget who I am.''

''Crown Prince Alexander?'' she asked tightly.

''A man who will never love you, Sophia.''

# Nine

"Aren't you supposed to be on your honeymoon, lass?"

"One would think," Sophia replied, stretching out in one of Ranen's bedraggled armchairs with Aggie, the large wolfhound pup, curled up on her lap. "I didn't know where else to go."

Ranen reached over to touch her hand, then quickly retreated. "You are always welcome here, lass, you know that."

She didn't, but was so thankful to hear it. For better or worse or somewhere in between, Ranen was family and the closest thing she had to her grandfather. She needed the strength of him and the consolation of his small, comfortably worn house right now.

"Would you like to tell me what happened?" he asked, filling a pipe with fragrant tobacco and setting it to light.

She shrugged to hide her discontent, but ended up spilling it, anyway. "It's Alex."

"Go on with yourself, lass."

"You know, I take this marriage very seriously."

"And you think the prince does not?"

"I think he takes the *union* seriously, but the marriage…" She sighed heavily. "I've fallen in love, Ranen."

"I know."

"But he won't allow himself to fall in love with me."

"Tosh. You're wrong about that, lass."

Hopes and wishes surged through her at his words, but she shook her head. "I don't think so. He's made it pretty plain."

At that, Aggie yawned, stretched, her front paw lifting into the air and dropping down directly on top of Sophia's hand. Sophia couldn't help but smile at the sweet, almost sympathetic gesture.

"He's fighting you because he's falling in love with you," Ranen said, pointing his pipe at her for emphasis.

Her heart, her senses, darted back to the glory of last night. Alex had been so giving, so wonderful. The way he'd touched her with such veneration, looked at her with such care. In those wondrous hours, he'd felt every inch her husband.

And though the ceremony and reception had been less than ideal, he had truly given her the perfect wedding night.

Perfect wedding night, she thought sadly, for one very imperfect couple.

"If that's true," she said softly. "If he's really fighting me because he's falling in love with me, who do you think will win in the end? The very controlled prince of Llandaron or his feelings of love?"

The question seemed to startle Ranen, and he leaned back against the unlit fireplace and harrumphed loudly. "Can't say. Can't rightly say. Both are worthy opponents."

Didn't she know it? Alex and his mind set were at odds almost daily. Sometimes she feared they would destroy each other, leaving no victors, no spoils.

The situation reminded her of those trials and tribulations of her mom and dad. Constantly at odds, no one winning, everyone losing.

"What is it, lass? You look a mite disconcerted."

Sophia spoke with quiet but desperate firmness. "I just want my child to come into a loving family, not like—"

"Yours?"

She nodded. "My parents hardly spoke to each other. They weren't even friends, Ranen."

"Don't fret anymore on it today, lass. Llandaron is a special place. Magic lurks here."

"I could use a little magic."

He raised a bushy eyebrow. "Well, it grabs hold of you when you need it most."

"Then why hasn't it found you?" The query came out in a rush, unprepared but honest.

A query that took Ranen completely unaware. "Me?"

Sophia saw the twinge of aloofness brush over Ranen's eyes, but she pushed on. He was her family; she cared for him deeply and she wanted him to be happy. "Looks to me like that Llandaron magic you're talking about has been trying to grab on to you for quite some time, but you keep running."

He simply glared at her, frowning.

"I'm not afraid of that look, Ranen. Your brother had a mighty fierce one of his own. And whenever I did something wrong, he gave it to me good. So, try something else."

"I think you've been eating too much of that taffy Fran and Catherine are so bloody keen on," he growled with frustration. "Clogged your brain, it has."

"This has nothing whatever to do with taffy, old man. It has to do with love."

"Love?"

"You love Fara."

Ranen's mouth fell open, and his pipe dropped to the floor.

"And Fara loves you."

"This is foolish talk—"

"I know she does."

"Tosh," he said impatiently.

She leaned forward. "You need to do something about it before it's too late."

"I know what I need and what I don't. And I don't need you coming here, telling me—"

The look of defiance Sophia shot his way made him stop where he was and listen to what she had to say. "Regret is an unhappy state of affairs, Ranen."

He shook his head. "The niece giving the great-uncle unsolicited counsel. It's…it's…"

"It's family, Ranen. And family is a blessing."

For a moment the old man only stared at her, and she wondered if he was going to order her out of his house. But then an amazing thing happened. Maybe it was a little of that Llandaron magic kicking in, who knew, but Ranen's face split, actually split into a wide, toothy grin, and he said, "You're a right winning lass, you are, Sophia."

The compliment touched her deeply, in that place left vacant by family long gone. And it fueled her, as well. To stick things out and make things right, make things better, best, with the man she loved.

All for the child she loved….

\* \* \*

He'd found her.

Finally.

He'd been to the beach house, the boat works, then to Ranen's place looking for her with absolutely no luck. Then, he'd come to town for a pint at the pub, and there she was. Out on the cobblestone sidewalk beside Gershins Taffy. One of the older palace guards was sitting beside her, and fifty or so town's children surrounded them.

At first Alex had wanted to go to her, but as he'd gotten closer to the crowd, he'd thought better of it. She was talking and laughing with the boys and girls, asking all about their favorite animals and what they'd like to see that animal do. Fly? Dance? Belch…? When she'd said that Alex had laughed so hard he'd nearly caught the attention of the group, so he'd backed up to a safe distance.

One thing was certain. The children adored her, wanted to be near her. She had a special rapport with them. He'd never seen anyone so willing to play without reserve or embarrassment before. Not even when he was a child himself.

She would be a wonderful mother to their child.

Alex felt his gut tighten. In seeing Sophia that way, he couldn't help but wonder what kind of father he would be when the time came.

It was at that moment that Sophia caught his eye. Alex flinched at the unease he saw in her gaze. She was probably wondering why he was there, whether for good or bad. But his presence obviously made her nervous and, he noticed with deep regret, made all of that brilliant childlike pleasure drain from her spirit.

He didn't blame her for reacting to him in such a way. After the magic of last night, then the boorish attitude he'd offered her this morning, he wouldn't blame her if she chose not to speak to him. But Sophia wasn't that sort. She was a brave, bold, gutsy creature. She would not ignore him or shame him by cutting him in front of his people.

After thanking the children and giving them all a winning smile, she disentangled herself from the group and walked over to him. Her guard followed but kept a respectful distance.

"Good afternoon, Your Highness."

He reached out, took her hand and kissed it. "And to you, Your Highness."

Her gaze tripped a little, and she eased her hand from his grasp.

"You looked like you were having fun," he said, trying to find an easy subject.

"The children are very sweet and very patient. They were helping me with my writing."

"Having some trouble focusing?"

"Yep."

Alex glanced around casually, just to see who observed them, then said in a low voice, "As am I, Sophia."

At his telling admission, she looked up at him with understanding, steady eyes. "What do you suggest we do about it? Stay away from each other?"

He could feel her anger, her frustration and felt ashamed for having been the cause. "That's not very practical, is it?"

"Not really."

Around them the people of Llandaron were beginning to stop and stare. Under normal circumstances, like a drink or meal or shopping trip into town, his people gave the royal family a wide berth. But as this royal had just married their new princess the day before, they weren't being as generous.

Alex offered her his hand. "Shall we walk?"

After seeing the growing flock, she nodded. "All right."

With the palace guard trailing behind them, Alex led her down several streets until they arrived at Short Street, a charming, little way, quite private. He stopped and gestured to a white bench, whereupon Sophia sat and he followed suit.

"How about if we try not to think," Alex began, "or to reason anymore?"

When she turned to face him, surprise registered on her face. "Really?"

"Yes."

"What about false judgments, Alex?"

He stiffened at her frankness, but as it was deserved

he acquiesced. "I will abstain from all judgments, m'lady."

"For how long?"

He grinned. "As long as we can."

She smiled tentatively. "So, we don't think or reason, we just…"

"Experience."

"And enjoy."

"Yes."

"All right."

He took her hand again, smiled when she didn't pull away and said, "Will you come somewhere with me?"

"Where?"

"It's a surprise."

Sophia could hardly believe her eyes.

Before her on the computer screen was a tiny peanut-shaped object inside a wedge of blackness. At first she'd hardly seen it. But then, slowly, as the doctor moved the probe around her abdomen, the object had seemed to grow darker or lighter, somehow catching her eye, drawing her to it.

Sophia felt a lump in her throat, but she managed to say, "That's my child?"

Sitting beside the ultrasound monitor, the royal doctor nodded his head. "It's a bit early, but yes. This is your child, Your Highness."

Tears welled up in Sophia's eyes. She was no wilting flower, granted, but a life was growing inside her. One she and Alex had created together. And that statement was almost overwhelming because she loved him so much.

"And the heir to the throne of Llandaron," the doctor finished reverently.

She gave the doctor a nervous smile. Yes, her child would be heir. He or she would be a prince or princess of Llandaron.

How life had changed in a matter of mere weeks, she mused as Alex inched closer to her, his gaze fixated on the screen, his hand wrapping around hers. Five months ago she was alone, no family, few friends, no stories to tell. And now she had a husband, a family, an uncle, a country, a direction, a heart full of stories and, most important, a child.

Brow furrowed, Alex pointed to the screen. "What is that, Dr. Tandow?"

"The baby's heart, Your Highness."

Alex squeezed her hand, no doubt unaware that he was doing so. "It's beating rather fast. Is that—"

"It's perfectly normal, Your Highness," the doctor assured him.

"Beautiful," Sophia cooed.

"Yes, Your Highness."

Your Highness. Lord, would she ever get used to such a title? For it didn't suit her at all. A strange name for little, scrappy Sophia Dunhill from San Diego, who used to sit out on her grandfather's boat and drip Popsicle juice all over herself.

"I think I'll leave you both alone now." The doctor stood then, inclined his head. "Your Highnesses."

When the man had left the room and closed the door, Sophia turned and looked up at her prince. He looked so devilishly handsome in his black dress shirt and pants. His dark hair a bit mussed, his jaw slightly dusted with stubble, and that tan skin against those sexy amethyst eyes.

And he belonged to her.

He brushed a thumb over her cheek. "Good surprise?"

"The best. Thank you."

"Consider it an apology."

"For what?" She knew what he was apologizing for, but she wanted to hear him say it, needed to, deserved to. If they were ever going to get anywhere with this "no judgment, no thinking" plan of his, they needed to start with a clean slate.

He grinned. "My asinine behavior this morning."

She found it impossible not to return his alluring smile. "Ah, yes, that."

"Do you accept my apology?"

"Hmm," she began, feeling a rush of wickedness invade her blood. "I feel there should be some kind of punishment involved, don't you?"

He leaned down, gave her a soft, drugging, nipping

kiss that left her mouth and the lower half of her burning with fire.

"Was that the kind of punishment you meant, m'lady?" he asked huskily against her lips.

"You're certainly on the right track," Sophia uttered through a breathy chuckle.

"You require more?"

"Definitely."

"Kisses or…?" His hand moved under her blouse, up, up until his fingers brushed her lace-covered breast. "Caresses?"

She swallowed hard. "Caresses are good."

It was the most erotically romantic moment of her life. Crazy as it was. Never in a million years would she have thought that lying on a metal table, fully clothed, kissing her husband while the doctor waited outside and could walk in on them at any moment, was romantic.

But it was.

Wild and wickedly romantic.

After stealing a quick kiss, she whispered, "Maybe Dr. Tandow would let us borrow this room for say…an hour."

Alex smiled, his thumb sweeping lightly over her hardened nipple. "Although, the thought of staying like this, holding you, making love to your mouth for a good long time in this very public place sounds intriguing, I have plans for us."

"Plans? Wasn't this—"

"This was merely…an appetizer, Sophia."

"You mean an appe*teaser*."

A wide grin overtook his features before he broke into a full-on chuckle. "Why don't we go now?"

He helped her sit up. "Let's go back to the beach house and change into evening clothes. I'm taking you to dinner and a movie tonight."

"A date?"

"Indeed."

"Dinner, movie…then what?"

He leaned close, whispered in her ear, "More making up."

She shivered. "Making up or making out?"

He chuckled, the sound deep and rich. "You make me…"

"What?" she demanded, standing up before him. "Crazy?"

"No. Happy."

The word had come out fast, in a rush, unexpected and powerful. Alex looked appalled at what he'd allowed himself to say. But the word had been music to Sophia's ears, and she wasn't about to let him recant. So, before he could even open his mouth to speak, she grabbed his hand and pulled.

"Come on, Highness, let's get you home."

# Ten

---

**B**eside the rousing fire, tangled in silk sheets and each other, Alex pulled Sophia closer, reveling in the feel of her skin against his own. It was truly amazing how her curves and valleys fit him to perfection.

Satiated by their fierce lovemaking, yet growing needful once again, Alex gave her a soft kiss on the mouth and whispered, "Tell me."

She dragged her smooth thigh across his groin. "You'll laugh."

As her minor shift of position charmed the lower half of him into rock-hard erection, he uttered hoarsely, "Do I strike you as the kind of man who is moved easily to laughter?"

"Good point."

With a slash of smile, he again pulled her to him in a heady show of possessiveness that had him questioning his rapidly deteriorating self-control. Why couldn't he pull her close enough? he wondered. Like inside him, where his heart pounded and his blood pulsed only her rhythm? And why couldn't he get enough of her? It was maddening. He was Alexander Thorne, the man who would have control at all costs. And here he was relinquishing that power willingly.

But then, he'd promised not to think.

"Whatever it is, Sophia," he said, brushing his lips across her forehead. "I'll take care of it."

"All right." She sighed. "It's bread pudding with cream."

"Hmm." He glanced out the window at the predawn sky. "I might have to take care of that craving tomorrow."

"There's no pubs open after 3:00 a.m. in the village?"

"I'm afraid not. I could wake the palace, however."

"No, I wouldn't dream of doing something like that." She lifted her head to the top of his shoulder and nuzzled his neck. "It can wait until tomorrow."

Her touch, the genuine way she moved, made him weak. A man who knew few weaknesses was humbled by this amazingly beautiful redhead with her quick wit, sharp mind and loving tongue.

"Is there anything else you crave?" he asked.

At that, she eased up on her elbow, palm to chin, and gazed down at him. "What are you offering?"

Alex skimmed his thumb over her pouty lower lip and arrested the urge to taste her. At least for the moment…while she gazed at him in that way.

Bloody hell, did she have to look at him with such openness? As though she wanted to read the words on his soul? Why couldn't this romance have just remained easy and untroubled and fulfilling the way he'd suggested earlier in the day?

Because Sophia wasn't a woman to be content with "easy."

And he wasn't a man who had ever been fulfilled—not until she'd come along at any rate.

"Such suspense, Your Highness," she said softly, interrupting his thoughts, hauling him back to the present, back to her and the feel and smell and look of her.

His control fell, utterly lost now.

With one quick movement, he had her on top of him, sitting on top of him, her long, muscular legs straddling his waist. "I offer myself," he said, feeling her warmth, her silky wetness pressing against the head of his hard shaft. "But I expect my own craving to be satisfied, as well."

"Of course."

"And I crave something sweet."

Her smile was brazen. ''What do you have in mind?''

A growl escaped his lungs as he gripped her hips and hauled her toward him, her buttocks raking over his chest, then collarbone until she was close, so close to his waiting mouth.

Sophia felt helpless yet powerful at the same time. Tonight had been a groundbreaking experience. The way Alex had touched her, talked to her, made love to her—his soul had come along for the ride…whether he'd wanted it to or not.

She was no fool, however. She hadn't said a word about her observations. And she wouldn't. She would only relax and enjoy.

But right now, as Alex found her, opened the hot, aching center of her, relaxation was an impossible ambition.

Sophia sighed, deep in her throat, anticipation washing through her. What would he feel like? she wondered madly. What would it feel like when his mouth, his tongue touched her? No man had ever been this close. No man had ever taken her to such an intimate place.

Love intermingled with desire as she reveled in the fact that her husband, the man she loved, was the first.

Then her mind went blank as Alex gave her one hot, raking stroke with his tongue. Shivers of painful delight racked her senses. Heat, electric and throbbing, pulsated in her blood as she waited for more, more...

Then it came. Light, quick strokes, back and forth over the hardened peak nestled in her core.

"Alex..." she whispered breathlessly, wanting him to understand that she was all his, that he made her feel and cherish and crave like she never thought she could.

"I know, sweetheart. I know."

His hot breath against the wet, throbbing bundle of nerves he was so intimately ministering to had Sophia calling out. Alex gripped her buttocks tightly, but lightened his caress as wicked and wonderful shock-waves rippled through her. Coursed through her at a heady pace.

But she didn't wait for the delicious feeling to subside. Instead, Sophia pushed away from his grasp, lifted her hips and lowered onto him.

"Sophia..." he uttered, his voice turning ragged.

She sucked in a breath, feeling the steely heat of his erection inside of her. It was like going home every time. And she knew so assuredly with each touch that she'd found the mate to her heart.

If only Alex would realize it, too.

Her thoughts and the blues they brought with them were taken as Alex gripped her hips and shifted her forward, deepening his penetration.

Dawn broke before them on their sandy spot, the sun rising out of the ocean like a giant peach. Sophia snuggled closer to Alex under the blanket, letting the gentle morning breeze send her hair fluttering about them both.

Was it actually possible that life was coming together? she wondered, staring out at the calm sea with its docile waves.

There was no denying that she'd fallen for this whole fairy-tale land just as she had fallen for its first family. She was so thankful for the time and the care of her new sisters, for the welcome of her father-in-law and for the second chance she had to get to know her uncle.

But most of all she was thankful for the chance to be part of a family, part of Alex's family.

''What were you like as a child, Sophia?''

The question, and the timing of it, startled her. Not simply because she'd had thoughts of family before he'd asked it, but because she and Alex had remained silent for quite a long time.

It had been a half hour ago when Alex had suggested they go down to the beach. After making love a third time, they'd both been satiated, yet neither one of them had wished to sleep.

Perhaps they'd desired each other's company in another way, she'd thought.

So, naked and warm, and wrapped in an enormous blanket, they'd come to the water's edge. And here they sat together on the sand, just being close without words. That was, until now....

"As a child," she mused aloud. "I would say I was curious, and I always tried to follow through on what I started or what I made a commitment to. And I tried to be creative, as well."

"That sounds like you. But—"

"But?"

"I think you might be missing something."

She turned, quirked her brow questioningly. "Oh, really?"

He nodded, grinned, then spoke in a thick brogue, "Me thinks you were also a stubborn little lass."

"And what make you *thinks* so?"

He chuckled, low and deep. "Are you seriously asking me for examples, Sophia?"

"All right, all right," she confessed crossly. "I might've been a tad stubborn—"

"A tad?"

"Fine. I was stubborn. Stubborn as they come. Mule-like in my stubbornness. Happy?"

His mouth twitched with amusement. "Ecstatic."

Sophia laughed, shook her head. She loved talking to him this way, irreverently and relaxed. Like this, they were friends as well as lovers.

"You know what, though?" she said, snuggling closer to him inside the blanket. "Despite the aforementioned stubbornness, I always took time, whether it was the appropriate time or not, to dream."

With true gentleness, Alex eased them both back on the sand and gathered her in his arms, the blanket cushioning them from the elements. "And what did you dream about, Sophia?"

"The future." Of finding someone I could really love, someone like you, she wanted to say.

"And what did you see in your future?"

"Well, when I was five, I dreamed that I'd grow up to be the world's biggest Barbie collector." She laughed softly. "Then later, I thought about becoming a doctor or a therapist. But when I started writing stories, I knew that was it for me."

Alex was quiet for a moment, then he said, "You were fortunate to have lived your dream."

Tender ground, she knew, and she wasn't about to tread boorishly. "What were you like as a child, as if I even need to ask?"

"Don't be so smug. It could surprise you."

She snorted. "Try me."

"I was clever."

"Of course."

"Handsome."

"Naturally."

"And probably too bloody serious for my own good."

Sophia gave a mock gasp. "No!"

With a husky grumble, Alex was over her in seconds, his black hair mussed and gleaming in the morning light, his beautiful mouth firm and sensual. "Mocking the crown prince of Llandaron..."

Lifting her hips, pressing against his arousal, she whispered, "What'll that get me? Ten years in the stockade?"

"I think you need twenty to straighten you out," he growled with mock severity. "But I'll rethink the stockade."

"You have something else in mind?"

"Torture. Highly sensual, guaranteed to make you misbehave again...and again."

This game had her tied up in knots, every inch of her skin on fire, while the lower half of her pulsed with need. She had barely enough breath to utter, "I can live with that."

But Alex didn't shoot back another sexy quip. Nor did he slip inside her as she'd expected, hoped, wanted. Instead he grew solemn, thoughtful.

"Sophia?"

"Yes?"

"I want our child to dream."

The fraught statement nearly undid her, as did the earnest tone in her husband's voice. Tears formed behind her eyes, hot and emotional. But she pushed them back. Tears were not what Alex needed right now.

"He," she smiled, "or she *will* dream."

"We will make sure of it."

"Yes."

Alex lowered his head, gave her a slow, drowsy kiss. "Yes."

Wrapping her arms around his neck, Sophia tipped her chin up and just gazed into his eyes. She saw so much when he allowed her to; his heart, his pain, *his* dreams...

Then suddenly, from out of nowhere, she gasped. "I have the perfect idea for a story."

"What?"

"For my new story. I've been struggling, not sure if I'm writing the right story. But now I know. I know what the right story is, Alex."

He kissed her lips again, then her cheek, whispering in her ear, "I love to see you happy like this."

And I love you, she thought, closing her eyes, feeling his mouth rake over her skin as his hands explored the curve of her back and buttocks.

"You were the impetus to the idea, Your Highness," she whispered breathlessly.

His lips brushed the pulse points on her neck, then trailed downward over her collarbone to her breast. "I inspired you?"

"More than you'll ever know," she uttered hoarsely as her husband sacrificed their blanket, their refuge, to the wind and took her swollen nipple into his mouth.

"I'm proud of you, big brother."

"For seeking your advice on the best in nursery

finery?'' Alex asked Cathy as they entered Belles and Beaux, Llandaron's most exclusive shop for babies.

Of course, it was tradition for the heir to the throne of Llandaron to sleep in the royal bassinet, the linens made especially for the little prince or princess by the nuns of St. Augustine, who lived just an hour away on the eastern coast. And Alex would accept this gift with thanks. But he was determined to purchase a few things for his child on his own. A crib, blankets, a few toys. Maybe some books, as well. He wanted to read to his child. He'd been told that babies were capable of hearing outside the womb at five months, and he wanted to make sure that his child got to know his father's voice as soon as possible.

''I'm proud of you for taking such an interest in your child,'' Cathy said, tugging him from his thoughts, looping her arm through his and steering him around the shop. ''I never thought I'd see the day when you stepped foot in a baby store.''

''It's nothing to get roused about, Catherine,'' he said with a trace of irritation. ''Sophia's busy writing. I thought I'd help out, surprise her with a few things, that's all.''

''Tosh, as Ranen would say.'' Cathy laughed richly as she led him over to a display of handmade cribs. ''You want to please her, make her happy.''

''Catherine…'' he began, his tone laced with warning.

''Why be ashamed of it?''

"I'm not ashamed—"

"Good to hear it. Because, big brother, you're turning into a wonderful husband whether you want to or not."

The sweet scent of designer baby powder in the air seemed to intensify all at once, swirling around Alex. No doubt the sensation had been brought on by the word *husband*. In the past the word had made his heart harden in anger and bitterness. In the past he had given the word little credence as it had always represented another's control. But lately, around a certain redhead, the word had only puzzled him, made him question, made him wonder.

He turned to Cathy who was watching him intently and asked, "Do you think Sophia would prefer the white or this pale green?"

"What do *you* think she'd like?"

"Stop playing games, Catherine. I don't have infinite amounts of time to spend here."

"That's right," she said, fingering a very sweet pale-pink baby blanket. "Shouldn't you be working right now? I've never heard of you taking time off during a workday."

He tossed her a black glare. "You're really making me regret inviting you along."

She touched his shoulder, smiling gently. "I'm sorry. I don't mean to tease. It's just that..."

"What?"

"Have you realized yet that your dream has come true, Alex?"

"I don't know what you mean."

"About how that beautiful mermaid rose up out of the water, red hair shining, green eyes blazing, and with one look made you feel like a different person, like you could fly."

As a salesman walked discreetly past them, Alex lowered his voice to a harsh whisper. "I'm only going to say this one more time, it's not like that between Sophia and me."

"No?"

"No."

"What's it like, then?"

"We are married and we have a child coming."

"As simple as that?"

At this point Alex was fairly ready to put his fist through the blue-and-pink-checked wall. It wasn't that he hadn't observed all the similarities between his childish dreams and today's realties. God help him, he had. Only too often. But what did it all matter? So, he had found and married the woman of his dreams...

Alex came to a screeching halt in his mind. Where had that come from? How had he allowed such a thought to register? *Woman of his dreams...* Men like him didn't entertain such foolishness.

"What do you think of this bookcase?" he quickly

asked, hoping Catherine would let the previous subject lie. ''Shall I order the complete set?''

But she wouldn't let the subject lie. She took a step closer, her gaze riveted on him, her voice a whisper. ''She's not Patrice.''

''What?''

''She's not Patrice. And you're not the man who was unhappily married for five years anymore.''

He glared at her, frowning. ''I know this, Catherine.''

''I don't think you do, Alex. I think you carry the weight of that relationship around with you day and night. I think that you're afraid if you give yourself, all of yourself, to Sophia, and things go wrong, you won't be able to hold your head up this time.''

Frustration suddenly matured to scalding fury. Through clenched teeth, he replied sharply, ''I won't discuss this subject further.''

Catherine refused to back down. ''You haven't discussed it at all.''

''I don't know if I like this new, modern, speak-her-mind Catherine.''

''Well, get used to it, buddy.'' A glint of amusement tugged at her mouth as she tried to pull him out of his bad humor. ''Because you not only described me, but your sister-in-law *and* the most outspoken of them all—your wife.''

Again, Alex was stopped in his tracks. This time by a vision of Sophia. Gloriously naked beside him, wrapped in a blanket, her hair down and wild, her eyes bright with exasperation as he jested with her about her stubborn nature.

Just the thought made his bones ache for her.

"She is a stubborn lass, isn't she?" he muttered to himself.

But Catherine heard him and chuckled. "My poor Alex. You've really gone and lost your heart."

Grimacing, he returned to the gentle sparring they enjoyed so much. "What I've lost is my head when I called and asked you along today. Now, are you going to help with this or not?"

"Sophia would love the pale green." She leaned up and gave him a peck on the cheek. "But something tells me you already knew that."

Alex gave her a mock snarl, then turned to call over the salesman.

# Eleven

The cup of tea to Sophia's left was untouched and growing colder by the second. But it was a welcome sight. It was the first time since her grandfather's death that tea or a muffin or whatever she happened to have sitting beside her writing pad wasn't thoroughly consumed before she'd written her first sentence.

But not today. In fact, not any day this week.

*...Della Denkins passed out just three dreams that night. But every child she blessed woke up full of hope, full of happiness and full of heart.*

Sophia glanced up from the kitchen table and her last ten pages of story with the oh-so-prized "The

End'' affixed to the bottom and smiled broadly. She'd done it. Almost a year of writer's block and she'd finished this story in just under a week.

A story she was so proud of. A story she would dedicate to her husband and to her child. For it was not a story about a talking animal this time or a lost boy looking for a new friend.

It was a story about dreams.

A sudden pang of hunger rose up to claim her, taking her mind off dreams for a moment in favor of reality. This intense empty-stomach feeling was something that was happening pretty often as of late. First the slight nausea, then a ravenous appetite. Both of which could never be ignored.

Oh, the joys of pregnancy, she mused with a smile as she stood up and went to the fridge. Two extra large sandwiches coming up. Alex did love peanut butter…

That morning he'd mentioned that he might be coming home for lunch if he finished up with the chancellor on time.

Sophia grabbed the jelly and peanut butter, then scooped up the bread from the counter. He'd be here. Just as he had every day this week. And just as they had every day this week, they'd share a sandwich and a story about what each of them had done that morning.

Time was being so kind to them. Wooing them along in a romantic haze. Every day they'd talk and laugh and share about what they wanted for their child. Every night they'd make love in Alex's bed, then afterward he'd pull her close and they'd fall right to sleep.

They were having a marriage. An honest-to-goodness marriage. And while Sophia was giving Alex time to feel and understand himself, he was giving her, and them, a chance.

Her heart full, Sophia went about her sandwich making. She pulled out two slices of bread from the bag and opened the jar of peanut butter.

But that was all she did.

A soft gasp suddenly escaped her throat and the smile of happiness from a moment ago died on her lips. Letting the jars and bread fall haphazardly back onto the counter, she doubled over in pain, gripping her belly as both sides of her abdomen shot off burning sparks.

Fear plunged into Sophia's very soul, threatening to drown her. But she fought the feeling and tried to calm herself, tried to breathe deeply as she prayed for the pain to subside.

But it didn't.

It only worsened.

Every muscle in her body clenched tight as panic gnawed away at her confidence. With each twinge, she felt as though she was being ripped apart, torn apart at the pelvis.

Her gaze clouded with tears as she inched toward

the table, reached for the phone. She had to get to someone, call for help.

*God, please don't let me lose this baby.*

Again pain blasted into her groin, and she retracted her arm, crying out.

"Sophia?"

Sophia barely heard the doorbell, barely heard the feminine call through the fog in her mind.

"Sophia? Are you home? It's me, Fran."

With every ounce of strength she had left, Sophia cried out for the one person she needed.

"Alex…"

Alex walked into the beach house with a grin on his normally sedate face. He couldn't help it. As it had been from the moment he'd seen her standing on the bow of her sloop, red hair wild and shimmering in the sun, he couldn't wait to see her again.

Perhaps someday that intensity of need would subside. He couldn't imagine it, but perhaps it would and he could return to being Prince Alexander—serious, focused and, alas, unromantic.

He dropped his briefcase at the door and exhaled heavily. If the truth be told, he didn't want to be that man anymore. He didn't like that man. Actually, he never had. Serious, focused and unromantic were what he'd had to be to survive his past.

But Sophia Dunhill Thorne had changed all that.

She had changed him.

"Honey, I'm home," he called, his grin turning a little wicked as he glanced around the living room looking for her.

Yesterday, when he'd walked through the door, Sophia had been sitting at the dining table, totally calm and totally nude. With an easy smile on her lips, she'd made him eat his entire sandwich before he'd been allowed to have...dessert.

Sheer torture.

Well, today, he'd brought *her* dessert instead. Her new favorite: bread pudding with cream. And with it he'd also brought the hope of feeding it to her, watching the sweet confection as it slipped between her full lips.

That was, if she could be found.

His grin widening, Alex stalked from room to room searching for her. As he entered each space, he imagined her waiting for him beneath the sheets in one of the bedrooms or in the bath, doused in suds.

But she was nowhere to be found, he soon realized, as he came to the last room and found it empty.

Slightly vexed, Alex rushed back to the kitchen, hunting the countertops and tables for a note. Perhaps she'd run to the store or set up a picnic on the beach. But surely he would have seen her on his way in, if she'd chosen the beach.

A foolish, premature fear twisted around his heart. One he'd managed to block over the past several weeks. He despised himself for allowing it to return now. But the thoughts came regardless, heedless.

Had he missed something? A sign that Sophia might be unhappy? In their marriage? In Llandaron? After all, she had fought the arrangement at first. And though she seemed in relatively good spirits, she *had* been a bit preoccupied this week.

But surely that was only about the book she was writing.

He plowed his hands through his hair. Of course it was about the writing. Bloody hell, he was losing it. She'd probably gone to pick up a special lunch or maybe she finished the manuscript early and went out to mail—

Alex stopped short as his gaze caught on the blinking light of his message service. Shaking his head at his previous stupidity, he rushed to it and depressed the button; fully ready to hear his wife's voice.

But the message wasn't from Sophia.

"Your Highness, it's around 11:00 a.m." The voice was distinctly male and older. "Your boat has been repaired. Kip had it all buffed and polished and towed to the slip as you requested. And don't you worry about provisions. I personally saw to it that she's all packed and ready for your journey."

The machine beeped. No more messages.

A cold knot pulsed in Alex's gut. And it grew tighter and tighter with each breath he took. He could actually feel his gaze turn hostile as he stared at the answering machine.

*She's all packed and ready for your journey.*

Like an ocean wave in a storm, his past came rushing back, battering his heart. His mind bombarded with visions, his muscles tensing just as they had when he'd walked into his town house in Scotland and found Patrice gone. No note, no nothing.

Just like today.

Iron fists closed around Alex's soul. Had he really abandoned his vow? Lost all perspective? Had he actually allowed himself to believe that Sophia cared for him, wanted him, was in love with him?

Obviously he had, he thought, seething with anger and humiliation at his lack of control.

But he would get it back—at all costs. He had to. Sophia was carrying his child. His child! And the heir to the throne of Llandaron. That child would remain with him always.

Alex slammed his fist on the counter, curses falling from his lips.

If Sophia wanted out, fine. But she wasn't about to take their child with her.

"Alex?"

Alex whirled toward the door, found Maxim standing there, his jaw tight, his gaze strained.

Alex's lips thinned in anger. Sent to break the bad news to the crown prince. He sniffed sharply. At least

Patrice had had the decency to send a priest instead of a family member when she'd run off.

"What do you want, Maxim?"

"I've been knocking for thirty seconds," Maxim said, a slight hesitation in his hawklike stare.

Alex had no time for his brother's anxiety. "Why didn't you just walk in, then?"

"I was. And I did. Listen, Alex, I have to tell you something. I was going to call, but I didn't want to leave a message and…wait, what's the—" Maxim's eyes narrowed, two deep lines of concern etched between his brows. "You look like you're ready to strangle someone."

Or sink a fist into Maxim if his little brother's jaw didn't cease this bloody small talk. "Do you know where Sophia is?" Alex fairly snapped.

His brother's gaze slipped.

"Speak up, Maxim, for crissakes!"

"Fran came over here to see her today, but when she got here—"

Alex cursed brutally. "I knew it."

"Knew what?"

"She's gone."

"What are you talking about?"

"She's left town, isn't that what you've come here to tell me?"

"Alex, maybe you should sit down."

"I don't want to sit down," Alex bellowed, stalking over to Maxim, jaw clenched. "Just tell me what the hell is going on."

Frowning, Maxim inclined his head. "Alex, Sophia's been taken to the hospital."

# Twelve

Ranen sat forward in the bedside chair, his face fixed with tension. "How are you feeling, lass?"

"Much better. The pain's subsided." Sophia shook her head. "Who could've thought that stretching ligaments could be so excruciating?" Easing herself up into a sitting position, she grinned at her great uncle. "You know Ranen, that's the tenth time you've asked me how I'm feeling in the last hour?"

"Pardon me for being worried about my kin," Ranen grumbled good-naturedly.

"Kin, huh? You're acknowledging that now, are you?"

"Tosh! Always have, lass."

"Ranen…"

"Well, not at the first meeting, that's true enough. But I got things right now, don't I?"

Sophia touched the vase of heather beside her hospital bed. "Yes, you do."

"Get on with things, that's what I say now."

"Glad to hear it."

"Me and my old goat of a brother were too damn stubborn to get on with things. I regret that. But it stops right here, you understand?"

A wave of melancholy moved through the private room, scratching at the door of Sophia's heart. "I want to, Ranen. What happened between you two?"

Ranen jerked to his feet, aged bones crackling as he went. "Robbie lived in Baratin until his thirteenth year. Along with our mother and me. It wasn't the happiest of times, mind you. Our father had passed just two years before, and we clung to our mother like a newborn colt to a mare." Ranen moved to the window and stared out. "But she hardly noticed us. She was never the same after my father died, off in her own world most of the time. Robbie and I tried everything we could think of to get her attention, but nothing worked. Nothing until…"

Sophia didn't want to push him, but she felt as though he might need it, as though he'd been holding on to this story and the anger in his heart for too long.

"What happened, Ranen?" she asked softly.

"It's a bleak ending, Sophia."

"Please."

A heaviness settled over the hospital room as Ranen continued. "Robbie had an idea. Let's get ourselves lost, he said. Then she'll be worried and come find us." Ranen's voice grew rough yet weary. "She did come looking. We used to love to play at the beach, and she knew it. It was a wet morning. She slipped on a bit of sea rock and hit her head."

"Oh, Ranen…"

"My aunt who had been living in America came to take us back with her. But I refused to go. I wouldn't leave Llandaron, and I begged Robbie not to go, either. But he said he couldn't stay after…"

"All these years you—"

"I blamed him for our mother's death." His voice broke in misery. "And I hated him for leaving me."

Sophia swallowed, bit back tears. "I am so dreadfully sorry, Ranen." She now, more than ever, understood why her grandfather was such a recluse, why he believed so fervently in living every moment, why he wanted to sail around Llandaron but never go ashore.

When her great-uncle turned to look at her, anger didn't light his eyes anymore. Only sadness. "Thank you, lass. 'Tis over now. I've made my peace with Robbie and with my own dim-witted ideas about the past. We both did what we felt was right."

"You're a very wise man, Ranen. I wish everyone were as forgiving about their past."

"You speak of the crown prince?"

Sophia didn't know what made her do it, maybe she needed the comfort of family or maybe Ranen was the one person who understood her pain right now, but she reached out for him.

Eyes downcast, he moved to the bedside and took her hand. "You sure do love the man, don't you?"

"Yes. More than anything. I just wish…"

"What, lass?"

She shook her head. "My wishes have grown redundant."

"That he would let himself love you?"

A smile tugged at her mouth. "Yes."

"He'll come around, lass. A tree doesn't always fall at first stroke."

She looked up at him with surprise, his words causing her to remember her past, a past filled with love and understanding. "Grandpa used to say that."

Ranen leaned over and kissed her on the forehead, his whiskers tickling her skin. "Who do you think taught it to him?"

"Hello, Sophia."

A beautiful princess with short gray hair and violet eyes moved into the hospital room with a grace she was born into.

Sophia smiled warmly. "Hi, Fara."

The older woman walked around the bed to stand beside Ranen, but her gaze never left Sophia. "You have more color, my dear."

"The doctor said I should be able to go home tomorrow."

"He wants to watch you overnight. Good man. I approve."

"Tosh," Ranen said on dusty chuckle. "She's right as rain, aren't you, lass?"

"Right as rain," Sophia assured them both with a wide grin.

Fara gave a tinkling little laugh, like sleigh bells, then addressed the man beside her. "We should let her rest, Ranen, dear."

Ranen, dear?

What in the world? And when had this happened? Sophia felt too stunned at the blatant endearment to speak her queries aloud. But when she saw Fara place her hand on Ranen's shoulder and he actually laid his hand over hers, she couldn't be stopped. "What's this all about, you two?"

Ranen only frowned, while Fara winked.

"Rest now. Information later," the older woman said ushering her beau out of the room. She called over her shoulder, "We'll bring Alexander to you just as soon as he arrives, my dear."

Sophia watched them go with a mixture of happiness and melancholy. There was nothing she wanted more for her uncle and her new aunt than to realize their feelings for each other and give in to the love of a lifetime.

It was just that their coming together now made

her pine, made her wonder. Would it be the same with Alex and her? Would they deny their feelings until they were old and gray and unsteady?

Or would the dreams for love, for a future, that they each carried in their hearts be allowed to walk free?

Fear unlike any he had ever known blistered Alex's heart as he shot out of the elevator and onto the hospital's fourth floor. He stalked down the hall toward Sophia's room and grabbed the first person he saw in the corridor.

"Ranen, how is she?"

"Calm yourself, Highness. She'll be fine."

"Fine? What the hell does that mean? Where's the doctor?"

"He's in with another patient." Ranen patted his godchild on the back. "Honestly, lad, she's perfectly well. She just had some rather severe pain in her ligaments, that's all. The wee one is stretching out the uterus, is what the doctor said. 'Tis perfectly normal, he said."

"Oh, thank God." Alex's gut unclenched slightly, and he released the breath he'd been holding all the way to the hospital.

It had been like some sort of conspiracy on the journey over. Satan's plan to drive him mad. Horrid traffic, no cell phone service, terrifying thoughts about loss and fear and words unspoken.

"I must see her." Jaw tight, Alex headed down the

hallway toward Sophia's room. He had much to say, much to apologize for, and it couldn't wait.

Ranen followed him. "Before you go in, I want a word with you."

Brushing off the old man's request, Alex muttered, "I don't have time. I want to see her now."

"You'll make the time, Alexander." And with that, Ranen grabbed Alex by the arm, stopping him dead in his tracks.

Alex whirled to face the man, his eyes no doubt as black as his mood. "What the devil is going on, Ranen? Is there something you're not telling me?"

"No. No. Sophia and the child are fine. As I said, it was just a little scare."

"Then what's this all about? I should be with her, not having a conversation—"

"Sit down and try to keep your mouth shut, can you do that?" the old man barked.

Alex just stood there for a moment, blank, stunned. No one spoke to him in such a way. No one but his father, at any rate. Then again, Ranen had always been every bit a second father to him.

Brushing aside the twinges of defiance that were clawing to get free, he did as he was bid. The bench behind him looked sturdy enough. He sat down and gave the older man an expectant look.

Ranen didn't sit beside him, but put a foot up on the bench and leaned in close. "If you don't love the girl, you should let her go."

"What the hell are you talking—"

"You know very well."

"I will never let her or my child go." Alex's voice was firm, final.

"You sound like a man making up for lost pride, Alexander."

"And you sound like a man who's trying to play the part of grandfather."

"Not trying, Alexander. Doing."

"Is that right?"

"That's right."

"When did this start?"

Ranen pushed away from the bench, but kept his voice low as hospital staff dashed to and fro around them. "Never mind when. She's my blood and I'm going to protect her."

"From what?" Alex demanded hotly. "From me?"

"If I have to."

Alex snorted.

Ranen put a hand on his godson's shoulder, his voice softening for the first time in a long time. "Would you want her going through life as you did? With a spouse who didn't love her?"

The words cut deep, deeper than Alex could've imagined. And they sent well-hidden questions into his mind, as well. What *did* he want for Sophia? He hadn't thought of it until now. He knew what he wanted from her, but *for* her...

Hell, he didn't want to think of it. Because if he did, he'd have to look closely at himself and the true desires of his heart.

His anger piqued, he narrowed his eyes at Ranen. "I will not take love advice from a man who has spent decades denying his own feelings."

The man didn't flinch one bit, didn't back off, either. "That's over now, son. Your aunt Fara knows my heart. I'm not letting fear take any more of my days or nights."

Alex jerked to his feet. He'd had enough conversation, enough lecturing, enough hearing about newly found fantasies. "Good for you," he said brusquely, his gaze impassive and cold. "Now will you let me pass?"

"Stupid…bullheaded…son of a…" Ranen muttered, shaking his head.

But he stepped aside and let Alex go.


Sophia was staring out the window when Alex walked into the room. But she quickly turned and found his gaze. At first glance she thought he looked angry, but as he drew closer, she realized it was angst that darkened his mood.

"Sophia." His voice wrapped around her like the sweetest, warmest of blankets.

"I'm so glad you're here, Alex."

He sat on the edge of the bed, reached for her hand,

then drew back. "I'm sorry I wasn't there when this happened."

"It's okay. I'm okay." Why wouldn't he touch her, she wondered. Why was he so distant and tense? Was it fear over losing the baby? Of course, it had to be. This child was everything to him. "Don't worry, the baby is just fine."

"I know, and I'm unbelievably relieved."

"Then why the long face?"

His eyes swept over her. "Sweetheart, I'm worried about *you*."

The endearment tugged at her heart. "Me?"

He shook his head, his tone heavy with frustration. "I thought I would have a heart attack on the way over here."

"That wouldn't have been good," she said with a soft smile. "Both of us in hospital."

"I'm serious, Sophia. You scared me to death."

With a quick exhale she asked, "Do you know why that is, Alex?"

"Of course I know why," he said, his voice strained. "I just told you how worried I was about you—"

"No." She gave him a patient smile. "*Why* you were so worried?"

"Sophia, I care about you, dammit!"

"And?"

"Well, you're the first person I've been able to talk to in a long time."

''What else.'' Sophia fought for calm, but it was incredibly difficult. Her heart's desire was sitting beside her finally opening up to her, finally revealing himself and his feelings, and she didn't want to interrupt the flow.

''You're wonderful, intelligent, funny.''

''Thank you.''

He nodded, absentmindedly took her hand. ''I enjoy your company. I can't imagine my days without you.''

She squeezed his hand and grinned wickedly. ''Or your nights?''

''That goes without saying.''

''Oh, Alex.'' Sophia couldn't stop the laughter that bubbled in her throat.

''What?''

''Don't you know what this means?''

Alex looked totally perplexed.

''You love me.''

Sophia had never seen a jaw drop so fast in her life. But the sight didn't bother her. She'd walked a long road with Alex, a long road to get to this place of pure honesty and no regret.

For weeks she'd sat on her hands, kept her mouth shut about her feelings and hopes that he would come to realize his own first.

And he had. In his way he had.

''Don't look so shocked,'' she said, pulling him

closer until his face was just inches from hers. "You love me, Prince Alexander and I love you."

"Sophia…"

"We were meant for each other, Alex. Look at our history. Your dream, my sailing in Scotland, then later on your stretch of beach. It's kismet."

"I don't believe in—"

She stopped him, kissing him softly on the lips. "Don't be afraid. We'll do this together. I'm not going anywhere." Again she kissed him, whispered against his lips, "I won't hurt you or humiliate you. Don't be afraid to love me, Alex."

His head fell back suddenly and he groaned. "I'm not afraid to love you."

"What?"

"I'm not afraid to love you, sweetheart. Not anymore. I gave up the need to always be in control because I love you so, lass. I've loved you from the first moment I saw you." He kissed her hungrily, then drew back. "I was just too stubborn and too bloody afraid to admit it to myself."

"Then what is it?"

"Dammit, Sophia," he growled, gathering her in his arms, pinning her with his fiery gaze. "I'm afraid you'll stop loving me."

Sophia stared at him, totally shocked by what he'd just said. "Alex, that's not possible."

"Anything's possible."

"Not that," she assured him, gripping his shoulders tightly. "You're my heart, you have to know that."

"I do know. But fear is a damaging beast. And when I heard the message on the machine from the boat works, I couldn't help but think—"

"You mean about the trip?"

"Yes."

Sophia released a breathy laugh, her heart soaring to the rooftops as her husband held her close on the stiff hospital bed mattress. "The trip is for us, Alex. I wanted you with me when I finished the last leg of grandpa's tour." She gave him a tender wink. "I thought it could be a second honeymoon."

"Or a first," he said on a lazy grin.

"Yes."

"I'm such an idiot."

"Hey, watch it!" she warned. "Idiot or not, you're talking about the man I love."

Alex lifted her hand to his mouth and kissed her palm. "Marry me again?"

She nodded. "Okay."

"Just you and me and our child on the beach where we first met in front of the waves and the sun and God."

As she looked into her husband's eyes, she saw her future, so clearly this time and so bright. There were more children for sisters and brothers and grandfathers and great uncles to bounce on their knees. There were holidays and wedding anniversaries. There was wondrous work, writing and giving. And there was family, with a husband who adored his wife and learned to show her just how much a little more every day.

"The beach sounds perfect," Sophia said, curving her lips. "Then we'll sail off into the sunrise?"

Alex released her hand, leaned in and cupped her face. "I love you."

"And I love you."

Turning around and easing back beside her on the bed, Alex gathered her in his arms once again. "Don't ever stop saying that."

"Never." Sophia snuggled close to her husband and let her head fall against his shoulder. "Never, my love."

# Epilogue

---

*Baratin*
*Spring*

On the bow of a docked *Daydream,* of that beautiful boat her grandfather had designed and built, Sophia touched her large belly and watched her beloved uncle wait for the woman of his dreams to walk down the deck toward him.

To everyone that had come to witness the event, it was truly a fairy-tale ending, a long time in the making. But to Sophia, it meant so much more. Ranen had come home, had welcomed the spirit and blessing of his brother and was finally finding happiness.

To Sophia, her family was now complete.

Beside her, Alex hugged her close and whispered in her ear, "Does this remind you of anything, sweetheart?"

Sophia smiled broadly. Just a few months back, she and Alex had renewed their vows at the beach as he'd wanted, with only God and their child in attendance. They'd broken with convention and written their vows themselves and given each other matching wedding bands engraved with the date. And the following day they had set off for Baratin to fulfill a promise accompanied by Ranen's wedding gift, his sweet wolfhound pup, Aggie.

Snatching Sophia's attention, the bridal march, played by two violists on the dock—two old friends of Ranen's—started up, and down the flower-trimmed pier walked a woman of such extraordinary beauty, she made everyone on the deck and on the pier stop and gasp. Dressed in a fitted white gown, Fara was finally taking what she wanted, what she deserved, and she'd never looked happier.

"She's so in love," whispered Fran, rocking her little girl in her arms as Ranen and Fara spoke their vows to the proud and beaming king, who was doing the ceremonial honors.

"She's one of us now," Sophia said softly.

Cathy nodded, giving her sleepy little baby a kiss on the forehead. "Looks like we all have our Prince Charming, doesn't it, ladies?"

Fran, Cathy and Sophia all glanced up at the dashing, roguish and undeniably sexy men at their sides and grinned.

And when Ranen took his bride in his arms for a kiss, each lady grabbed her prince and followed suit.

While all around them, the fog rolled in....

\*     \*     \*     \*     \*

**Your opinion is important to us!** Please take a few moments to share your thoughts with us about your experiences with Harlequin and Silhouette books. Your comments will be very useful in ensuring that we deliver books you love to read.
***Please take a few minutes to complete the questionnaire, then send it to us at the address below.***

---

Send your completed questionnaires to:
**Harlequin/Silhouette Reader Survey, P.O. Box 9046, Buffalo, NY 14269-9046**

---

1. As you may know, there are many different lines under the Harlequin and Silhouette brands. Each of the lines is listed below. Please check the box that most represents your reading habit for each line.

| Line | Currently read this line | Do not read this line | Not sure if I read this line |
|---|---|---|---|
| Harlequin American Romance | ❑ | ❑ | ❑ |
| Harlequin Duets | ❑ | ❑ | ❑ |
| Harlequin Romance | ❑ | ❑ | ❑ |
| Harlequin Historicals | ❑ | ❑ | ❑ |
| Harlequin Superromance | ❑ | ❑ | ❑ |
| Harlequin Intrigue | ❑ | ❑ | ❑ |
| Harlequin Presents | ❑ | ❑ | ❑ |
| Harlequin Temptation | ❑ | ❑ | ❑ |
| Harlequin Blaze | ❑ | ❑ | ❑ |
| Silhouette Special Edition | ❑ | ❑ | ❑ |
| Silhouette Romance | ❑ | ❑ | ❑ |
| Silhouette Intimate Moments | ❑ | ❑ | ❑ |
| Silhouette Desire | ❑ | ❑ | ❑ |

2. Which of the following best describes why you bought *this book?* One answer only, please.

| | | | |
|---|---|---|---|
| the picture on the cover | ❑ | the title | ❑ |
| the author | ❑ | the line is one I read often | ❑ |
| part of a miniseries | ❑ | saw an ad in another book | ❑ |
| saw an ad in a magazine/newsletter | ❑ | a friend told me about it | ❑ |
| I borrowed/was given this book | ❑ | other: _____ | ❑ |

3. Where did you buy *this book?* One answer only, please.

| | | | |
|---|---|---|---|
| at Barnes & Noble | ❑ | at a grocery store | ❑ |
| at Waldenbooks | ❑ | at a drugstore | ❑ |
| at Borders | ❑ | on eHarlequin.com Web site | ❑ |
| at another bookstore | ❑ | from another Web site | ❑ |
| at Wal-Mart | ❑ | Harlequin/Silhouette Reader | |
| at Target | ❑ | Service/through the mail | ❑ |
| at Kmart | ❑ | used books from anywhere | ❑ |
| at another department store or mass merchandiser | ❑ | I borrowed/was given this book | ❑ |

4. On average, how many Harlequin and Silhouette books do you buy at one time?

| | |
|---|---|
| I buy _____ books at one time | ❑ |
| I rarely buy a book | ❑ |

MRQ403SD-1A

5. How many times per month do you shop for any *Harlequin and/or Silhouette* books?
   One answer only, please.

| | | | |
|---|---|---|---|
| 1 or more times a week | ❑ | a few times per year | ❑ |
| 1 to 3 times per month | ❑ | less often than once a year | ❑ |
| 1 to 2 times every 3 months | ❑ | never | ❑ |

6. When you think of your ideal heroine, which *one* statement describes her the best?
   One answer only, please.

| | | | |
|---|---|---|---|
| She's a woman who is strong-willed | | She's a desirable woman | ❑ |
| She's a woman who is needed by others | ❑ | She's a powerful woman | ❑ |
| She's a woman who is taken care of | ❑ | She's a passionate woman | ❑ |
| She's an adventurous woman | ❑ | She's a sensitive woman | ❑ |

7. The following statements describe types or genres of books that you may be
   interested in reading. Pick *up to 2 types* of books that you are most interested in.

   I like to read about truly romantic relationships ❑
   I like to read stories that are sexy romances ❑
   I like to read romantic comedies ❑
   I like to read a romantic mystery/suspense ❑
   I like to read about romantic adventures ❑
   I like to read romance stories that involve family ❑
   I like to read about a romance in times or places that I have never seen ❑
   Other: _____ ❑

*The following questions help us to group your answers with those readers who are
similar to you. Your answers will remain confidential.*

8. Please record your year of birth below.
   19 _____

9. What is your marital status?
   single ❑   married ❑   common-law ❑   widowed ❑
   divorced/separated ❑

10. Do you have children 18 years of age or younger currently living at home?
    yes ❑   no ❑

11. Which of the following best describes your employment status?
    employed full-time or part-time ❑   homemaker ❑   student ❑
    retired ❑   unemployed ❑

12. Do you have access to the Internet from either home or work?
    yes ❑   no ❑

13. Have you ever visited eHarlequin.com?
    yes ❑   no ❑

14. What state do you live in?
    _____

15. Are you a member of Harlequin/Silhouette Reader Service?
    yes ❑   Account # _____   no ❑   MRQ403SD-1B

# COMING NEXT MONTH

**#1537 MAN IN CONTROL—Diana Palmer**
*Long, Tall Texans*
Undercover agent Alexander Cobb joined forces with his sworn enemy Jodie Clayburn to crack a case. Surprisingly, working together proved to be the easy part. The trouble they faced was fighting the fiery attraction that threatened to consume them both!

**#1538 BORN TO BE WILD—Anne Marie Winston**
*Dynasties: The Barones*
Celia Papleo had been just a girl when Reese Barone sailed out of her life, leaving her heart shattered. But now she was all woman—and more than a match for the wealthy man who tempted her again. Could a night of passion erase the misunderstandings of the past?

**#1539 TEMPTING THE TYCOON—Cindy Gerard**
Helping women find their happily-ever-afters was wedding planner Rachel Matthew's trade. But she refused to risk her own heart. That didn't stop roguishly charming millionaire lawyer Nate McGrory from wanting to claim her for himself…and envisioning her icy facade turing to molten lava at his touch!

**#1540 LONETREE RANCHERS: MORGAN—Kathie DeNosky**
Owning the most successful ranch in Wyoming was Morgan Wakefield's dream. And it was now within his grasp—as long as he wed Samantha Peterson. Their marriage was strictly a business arrangement—but it didn't stem the desire they felt when together….

**#1541 HAVING THE BEST MAN'S BABY—Shawna Delacorte**
For Jean Summerfield, the one thing worse than having to wear a bridesmaid dress was facing her unreliable ex, best man Ry Collier. But Jean's dormant desire sparked to life at Ry's touch. Would Ry stay to face the consequences of their passion, or leave her burned once more?

**#1542 COWBOY'S MILLION-DOLLAR SECRET—**
**Emilie Rose**
Charismatic cowboy Patrick Lander knew exactly who he was—until virginal beauty Leanna Jensen brought news that Patrick would inherit his biological father's multimillion-dollar estate! The revelation threw Patrick's settled life into chaos—but paled compared to the emotions Leanna aroused in him.

SDCNM0903